CRESCENT MOON

TRIPLE MOON TRILOGY

BOOK 1

MADISON GRANGER

Crescent Moon, Triple Moon Trilogy, #1
By Madison Granger

This is a work of fiction. Names, characters, places, events, and incidents are either the product of the author's imagination or used in a fictional manner. Any resemblance to actual persons, living or dead, or actual events is purely coincidental.

This is an adult paranormal romance with love scenes and mature situations. It is only intended for adult readers over the age of 18.

Cover design finished by AK Designs, 2023

ISBN: 9798397204552
ASIN: B0C1HJ637B

Dedication

To my tribe.
I keep going because of you.

Acknowledgments

Sandy Ebel of Personal Touch Editing
The woman who continues to polish all my rough edges, making my stories shine with a magic of their own.

Angelina Kerner of AK Designs
Who came to my rescue, finishing the cover for me.

Ashley and Annie, my beta readers
Who gave me honest and helpful feedback.

The Crescent Moon signifies love and fertility.
It's also a time of patience and change,
or starting a new chapter in your life.

1

“I’ll pay you good money, Dr. Adkins. Any amount... name your price.”

“Mrs. Baker, we’ve been through this countless times. I run a veterinarian clinic, not a boarding facility. You have to take your dog home. There’s nothing wrong with him.”

“But I can’t walk him outside in this weather!” she sputtered. “I can’t keep up with him. Surely, you can make an exception.”

Nova didn’t even try to stifle her sigh. Maggie Baker was on her last nerve, and she found herself not even caring if she lost business because of the woman.

"I warned you before you bought Max that boxers were very energetic and that you would have problems containing him. You didn't want to hear it." Nova didn't bother with the unspoken *I told you so*. The message was clear.

"I thought veterinarians were supposed to be compassionate," the old woman sniffed.

"I *am* compassionate, Mrs. Baker, but I'm also not keeping your perfectly healthy dog in my clinic because you don't want to walk him in the snow. This one is on you. Now, if you'll excuse me, I have to close up and get home before the storm moves in. I suggest you do the same."

Opening the door, she motioned to Mrs. Baker to leave... *with* her dog. Max tugged on his leash, and the woman had no choice but to exit the clinic. With a muttered oath, Nova turned the latch on the deadbolt and the *Open* sign around. Glancing at the clock on the wall, she groaned. She'd lost valuable time arguing with the woman, time she needed to prepare for the incoming weather.

Praying there wouldn't be a crush of last-minute shoppers, Nova aimed her Jeep toward the grocery store. She was well-stocked at the cabin, previous winters had taught her well, but there were a few comfort foods she'd like to buy. Pulling into the near-empty parking lot, she sent up a prayer of thanks. Sprinting up and down the aisles, Nova was positively giddy as she loaded her basket. She would hibernate in style. Pulling two bottles of wine from the shelf, with a shrug, she reached for a third. What went better with a stack of books than a chilled glass of wine?

Nova loaded the last of the supplies into the back of the SUV. Exhaling a puff of cold air, she mentally ticked off her list before making the trek up the mountain. The Jeep had been topped off at the station, groceries to last a couple of weeks were in the vehicle, and the clinic had been shut down and locked up.

She'd left a message on her voice mail and on the clinic door saying she was closed except for dire emergencies. Nova prayed there wouldn't be any animal crisis—Mrs. Baker and Max included—to pull her from the warm, cozy cabin she owned in the Bighorn mountains. Considering the spotty, if nonexistent, cell service, anyone would be lucky to reach her.

Gazing up at the gray sky, she shivered. The large, puffy cumulus clouds were only one of the warning signs of the coming storm. Nova wanted to be home in front of a roaring fireplace, not stuck in a blizzard.

Sliding onto the driver's seat, she shrugged off her down jacket and pulled off thick, insulated gloves. Starting the Grand Cherokee while she loaded the groceries meant it was nice and toasty as Nova cautiously eased down the road.

By the time she'd traveled the fifteen miles to her cabin, all Nova could think about was she probably should've bought more wine. Her shoulders and back were knotted with tension from the drive up. Usually an easy drive, weather conditions had worsened by the time she'd reached the mountains. Snow was falling faster, making visibility a challenge.

Rounding the bend leading to her cabin was a welcome sight. It was already dusk, and she still had to unload the Jeep and haul more firewood to the house. Not for the first time, Nova was grateful for the garage situated close to the cabin, which was big enough for her vehicle and a good supply of firewood.

Forty-five minutes later, Nova had the fireplace going and was preparing a steak for dinner when the phone rang. She smiled as she glanced at the display screen.

"Hi, Dad."

"Hello, Nova. Did you have any trouble getting home?"

"Not too much. Thankfully I was almost home by the time the snow got heavier. I'm locked up tight with plans for sharing the evening with a good book."

"Sounds like a plan. One less thing I have to worry about." Jace Adkins chuckled at his daughter's response.

"Dad, I'm a grown woman. I can take care of myself."

"Yes, I'm aware, but I'm still your father and your Alpha. I have every right to worry about my eldest."

Nova rolled her eyes, grateful he couldn't see it.

"How's Mom and Reagan? Have you heard from Lena lately?"

The sigh over the line spoke volumes. Apparently, her youngest sister was still MIA. Lena had a wild streak and was always off on a new adventure.

"Your mother and Reagan are fine. Both send their love." Murmuring in the background interrupted him for a moment. "Mom said to that you're excused from dinner this weekend, but she expects to see you as soon as the weather clears."

"I'll be there as soon as I can," Nova assured her father. "I promise."

"Fair enough. I won't keep you any longer but call if you need anything. I can send Bryce and Linc out on a moment's notice."

"I appreciate it, but I'll be fine. Keep your enforcers at home. They don't need to be traipsing all over the countryside in this weather." Nova bit her bottom lip, debating on bringing it up again, but her father wasn't the only one who worried about the youngest of the Adkins family. "Dad, where's Lena?"

"I'm not sure, sweetheart. Last I heard, she was on her way to California. She hasn't called in a couple of weeks and her phone always goes to voice mail. I'm trying to let her lead her own life, but it's hard on us, especially your mom."

"It's not like she's a kid, Dad. I'm sure she's fine, but I know what you mean... we all worry about her."

"I'm way too young for the gray hair that one has given me," Jace sighed. "At least you and Reagan have good heads on your shoulders. Remember to call if you need anything."

"I will, and thanks. Love you, Dad."

"Love you too, sweetheart."

Nova put the phone back on the charger. Her youngest sister was going to drive their parents nuts with her crazy adventures. Lena followed her own path, with little regard to how it affected her family. At least she wasn't getting into trouble... that they knew of.

Glancing at the firewood rack, Nova bundled up and grabbed the log tote. It was overkill, but she'd rather get more wood now than have to do it first thing in the morning.

The wind whipped around Nova as she struggled to cover the short distance to the garage. She was grateful she'd splurged on the extra-large outbuilding, giving her plenty of room for multiple cords of firewood. Checking for snakes and other critters nesting in the wood was part of a regular routine, but in this weather, she'd give them what comfort they could find as long as they left her alone.

As she stepped outside, a scream of pain caught her attention. She tried to pinpoint where the sound had come from, but the howling wind distorted everything. It sounded more human than animal, but what would anyone be doing out in this blizzard? Nova waited for more sounds, but none came. Figuring it was only the wind and her overactive imagination, she made her way back to the house.

Once inside, she tended to the fire and dimmed all the lights except for the lamp next to her favorite chair. Wrapping a throw around her, she opened the first book from the stack she planned on reading while the storm kept her indoors. She was only a few pages in when she felt her eyelids get heavy.

Pounding on the door jerked Nova awake, her book falling to the floor. Shaking her head to wake herself, she stumbled toward the door. The clock on the mantel read two a.m. She must have dozed off around midnight. The pounding became more insistent, so Nova shook off the last vestiges of sleep and sprinted to the door.

Pulling the door open, she found a man carrying another, thrown over his shoulder. Both were bundled against the cold, but even the wind and snow couldn't disguise the metallic smell of blood.

"I need help... bear trap..." the stranger gasped.

Nova didn't hesitate, opening the door wider for the man. This wasn't the first time someone had shown up at her door with injuries. Most of the residents on the mountain were shifters of some kind, and her reputation as a veterinarian and healer was widespread.

"Bring him in here so I can look at his wounds."

Nova led them to one of the guestrooms, hurrying to pull the sheets back on the bed. Together, they laid the man down, stripping him of outer wear and wet clothing. It was then Nova saw all the blood from a jagged tear and gaping puncture wounds on the man's leg.

"I'll be right back. I need towels and my medical bag."

"You're a doctor?" Relief was visible in his light green eyes.

"I'm a vet, but I can deal with this," Nova assured him.

Hurrying from the room, she grabbed the needed supplies. Nova had the means to clean and stitch the wound. She'd have to improvise if there was severe damage to the leg, but it was the lack of medicine she worried about. Nova didn't have antibiotics or pain pills on hand.

Returning to the room laden with supplies, the stranger helped her clean the patient's wounds and passed her what she needed.

"Thank you for letting us in. I don't know what I would've done if I hadn't seen your place. My truck is at the base of the mountain. We hiked up here this morning."

"What in the world possessed you to go hiking in this weather? Weren't you aware there was a blizzard moving in?"

The bearded man had the grace to look embarrassed.

"We weren't supposed to be up here this long. Landon wanted to get some winter shots… he's a freelance photographer, and I wouldn't let him come up here alone. It was supposed to be only for a few hours, but he found some tracks…"

"And one thing led to another, I suppose?" Nova finished for him.

"Yeah, something like that." He shrugged. "It wasn't one of my better moves. I'm just thankful you were here." He gave her a half-smile. "I'm Sawyer, by the way. Sawyer Billings. And this is Landon Monroe."

"Nova Adkins." She held up a hand covered in blood. "I'll shake your hand after I get cleaned up."

"Not a problem." Sawyer held his own hands up, which weren't much cleaner than hers. "I think we passed the opportunity for proper introductions."

"You might have a point," Nova agreed as she surveyed her work. "Your friend got lucky. He sustained some nasty cuts and deep puncture wounds, but I don't detect any broken bones, and the bleeding is under control, so no extensive damage there." She glanced at Sawyer from under hooded lids. Nova couldn't help but notice how attractive the man was, despite being dirty, disheveled, and obviously exhausted. "A couple of shifts and he should be good as new."

"Figured it out, huh?"

Nova pointed at the side of her nose.

"Kind of hard to miss, though you two aren't from around here. I don't suppose you bothered to check in with the local Alpha before you went hiking around his territory?"

Sawyer went still, his face paling despite a tanned complexion.

"You must think I'm all kinds of stupid," he said softly.

"I'm not one to judge so fast, and I'm sure there's a story. Since we're going to be cabin bound for a few days, I have time for a long tale." She pulled her gloves off with a snap. "I don't have any meds with me, so Landon is going to have to tough it out. Luckily, he's a shifter, so the healing process shouldn't be too rough. Let him rest for now. How about we clean up, then I'll fix us something to eat?"

"You got yourself a deal."

2

Nova seasoned two steaks while the skillet heated. She tried to do some quick math in her head, figuring out how long her food would last with two extra mouths to feed. If the storm didn't keep them cabin-bound for more than a week, she might be able to stretch things. Luckily, she always kept the place well-stocked, especially in the winter. Her mother had taught her well.

"You mentioned that Landon is a photographer. What do you do?" Nova asked as she prepared the meal. "There's some beer in the fridge if you want one."

"Thanks, appreciate it." Sawyer eased around the kitchen to the refrigerator. "Want one?" At a shake of her head, he opened it and took a long pull. “Hard to believe a cold beer could be so good with a blizzard howling outside.” He tossed the bottle cap into the garbage can and pulled out a bar stool. “I’m a business consultant.”

“A freelance photographer and a business consultant?” Nova’s brow arched. “How did you two get together?”

“It’s not like that.” Sawyer snorted. “Landon was abandoned as a baby, and my parents took him in and raised him as their own. I was ten at the time, and he’s been my kid brother and best friend ever since.”

“But you have different last names… your parents didn’t adopt him?” Nova glanced at him over her shoulder. “If I’m being too personal, just stop me.”

“It’s all good. Landon’s father was friends with my parents. His dad was killed overseas, and his mom couldn’t handle raising a pup on her own.” Sawyer shrugged. “One night she took off, and we found Landon on our front porch, bundled up in a basket. He was only a month or two old. Dad wanted Landon to know who his father was, so they never changed his last name to ours.”

“He’s lucky to have landed with such a loving family,” Nova observed.

“It worked out for everyone. Mom and Dad always wanted more pups, but they only had me. Landon was an answer to a prayer for them, and I got an awesome little brother in the bargain. He’s my best friend and we still do everything together.” Sawyer tossed his empty bottle into the garbage. "Is there anything I can do to help?"

"You can grab a couple of plates from that cabinet." Nova pointed with her fork. "These will be ready in a few minutes."

"What about you? Any siblings?"

"Yeah." Nova grinned. "Two sisters. I'm the oldest. Reagan is a teacher and Lena is… finding herself."

"Got ya." Sawyer laughed. "Most of us have gone that route at one time or another."

"Everyone but me and Reagan, it seems." Nova smiled ruefully. "It's hard not to follow the rules when your father is the Alpha of the pack."

"Oh, shit," Sawyer breathed. "Your dad is Alpha of the Bighorn Mountain pack?"

"That would be him." Nova tucked a lock of silver hair behind her ear, an amused smile on her face.

"What was it like… growing up in an Alpha's home?"

"No different from anyone else's life, I imagine." Nova mulled over her answer for a moment. "Dad was strict, but not unreasonable. He and Mom are Fated Mates, so there's a lot of love in our home."

"Sounds a lot like mine, only difference being we were simply pack members and my parents weren't Fated Mates, but they loved each other enough to stay together."

"There's nothing wrong with that." Nova smiled at him as she set the plates on the table. "You didn't have to deal with the pressure of being the Alpha's kid."

"True enough. Landon and I grew up about as normal as a couple of wolf shifters could." Sawyer swallowed his steak. "This is amazing! And she cooks too!"

"I have all kinds of talents." Nova laughed. "Tell me, though, what brings the two of you here?" Her curiosity was piqued. "Shifters don't usually stray from their packs."

Being the oldest, her father had taught her shifter law and the ropes of leading a pack, in the event she would have to take over as Alpha. It wasn't a position she looked forward to, but she wouldn't shirk her duty. Her father was open-minded enough to realize a female was totally as capable as a male to lead a pack. There were a lot of alphas who didn't think that way.

"Too many alphas in a small pack," Sawyer said on a sigh. "Every day was a test to prove ourselves. Landon only wanted to take pictures, and I never understood the reason to have to prove myself." Sawyer collected their empty plates and brought them to the sink. "We're both freelancing, so we took to the road. When I had to drop into a town to do a job, Landon would do photo shoots nearby. It's been working well enough for us."

"Which kind of brings me back to the here and now. Do you think you could show me where the bear trap is? My dad needs to know about this. He's going to have a field day with the local sheriff."

"I can try. The storm has already covered any tracks I made getting here, but I've got a decent sense of direction."

While talking, Sawyer had washed the dishes while Nova cleared off the table and wiped everything down. She was comfortable around the shifter and enjoyed talking to him. Nova couldn't remember the last time she'd been this relaxed around a male other than her father and his men. She'd always been the serious one, focused on her studies, instead of hanging out and flirting with the males. Relationships had been few and never lasted long.

"I want to check on Landon before I turn in. There's another bedroom next to the one he's in that you're welcome to use."

"Thanks, I appreciate it. Hopefully, we won't be in your hair very long."

"Your brother should be up and about in a couple of days," Nova assured him. "We'll have to see how the weather holds, though." Tossing the dishtowel to the counter, she turned and bumped into Sawyer, not realizing he'd been that close to her. The contact between them was like an electrical charge and for a split second, Nova lost her breath, her eyes widening in wonder.

"Tell me you felt that," Sawyer rasped.

"Yeah, totally didn't see that coming." Nova stood still as a statue, not believing what her wolf was excitedly telling her. Sawyer was her Fated Mate, something she wasn't prepared for at all.

Sawyer stepped toward her, and Nova backed, hands up.

"Whoa." Nova's voice came out shaky. She cleared her throat in an attempt to sound somewhat composed. "I'm not denying what just happened or what my wolf is telling me, but it doesn't mean I'm going to jump into your arms or bed simply because we're Fated Mates." Nova didn't miss the look of disappointment in Sawyer's eyes. She was also having a devil of a time ignoring the frustrated whine of her wolf.

"You're right, I'm sorry." Sawyer raked through his beard in agitation. "I never expected to find my Fated Mate, especially like this. Should've figured it wouldn't be smooth sailing."

"What do you mean?" Nova asked, curious in spite of herself about his wording.

"I'm sorry, I'm not real sure, to be honest." He gave her a rueful smile. "It's been a hell of a long day on top of a rough week. I thought finding one's Fated Mate was supposed to be this incredible insta-forever love." He ran his fingers through his hair. "Now I'm sounding like an idiot. How does this work, anyway?"

"Can't say for sure. Never had one before." Nova chuckled under her breath. "I'm reasonably sure the connection is instantaneous, but the rest comes in time." She couldn't fault him in the least because the same thoughts were running through her head. She'd been on her own for a long time and wasn't used to jumping in without testing the waters first... even with her Fated Mate.

She put a hand on his arm and the current went straight to her core. Sawyer covered her hand with his own, staring deep into her eyes.

"I'm not going anywhere, Sawyer, but I just met you. We have time to figure this out. Right?"

He nodded, not breaking the contact between them.

"Let's check on Landon, then get some rest. One day at a time, okay?"

Sawyer brushed her cheek with the pad of his thumb.

"I can live with that."

As Nova and Sawyer entered Landon's bedroom, she knew immediately something was seriously wrong. Landon was moaning and thrashing about in the bed, his skin slick with sweat.

"We need to calm him down so I can check his wounds." She gave Sawyer a worried look. "He shouldn't be reacting like this. I don't want him to tear his stitches open. Without shifting, he hasn't had a chance to start healing."

With Sawyer's help, Nova was able to remove the bloody bandages. As she suspected, he'd torn a few of the stitches and she would have to redo them. But they had bigger problems on their hands and her mind raced as she tried to figure out how to treat her patient.

"What are those black streaks on his leg?" Sawyer asked.

"If I'm right, it's silver poisoning," Nova replied.

"I was under the impression bear traps were made of steel."

"They are, unless someone tampered with it and laced it with silver." Nova methodically cleaned Landon's leg while she spoke.

"Can you save him, Nova?" Sawyer's voice was tight with fear.

"I'm going to do all I can."

Landon started retching, and Nova grabbed a small wastebasket by the bed in the nick of time.

"I need to get an anti-hemotoxin into his system before his organs shut down. We don't have much time."

"Where are you going to get that?" Sawyer asked. "You said you didn't have any meds here."

"I don't, not the everyday meds I use at work, but this is different. I always keep some on hand for situations like this. I've dealt with silver poisoning more than once." Nova gave instructions over her shoulder as she hurried from the room. "Try to keep him still. I'll be right back."

Sprinting up the stairs, Nova dashed to the bathroom connected to her bedroom. There were three bottles of an anti-hemotoxin in the cabinet, which should be enough to do the job. Swiping all the bottles from the shelf, she hurried back downstairs. Within minutes, she'd injected the first dose.

"Now what?"

"Now, we wait," Nova replied. "If I caught it in time, he'll start to respond soon." She glanced at Sawyer, who appeared as haggard as she felt. "Why don't you get some rest? I'm going to stay with Landon the rest of the night."

She could tell he was torn, wanting to stay with his brother, and needing to rest. Nova knew when the exhaustion won.

"Only if you promise to come get me if you need anything. I mean it."

"I will. Get some sleep, Sawyer." She smiled wearily. "I don't need you falling out on me, too."

"Thank you, Nova. I don't know what I would have done if it hadn't been for you."

"You have to admit, Fate got a little dramatic about getting us together."

Sawyer laughed softly.

"No kidding." He walked over to her and kissed her forehead. "Good night, Nova."

"Rest well," she replied softly.

Today had been full of surprises, a jumble of good and bad. Nova hoped there weren't anymore.

3

Sawyer stretched out on the bed, staring at the ceiling. A stupid misstep and Landon was fighting for his life. Trying to find help, he'd met his Fated Mate. What should have been a joyous moment was clouded with fear and despair. His life had never been a smooth journey, but this was taking it to extremes.

Throwing back the blankets, Sawyer got up and pulled on a pair of sweats from his backpack. He'd managed to doze off but woke with a start, once again hearing the anguished scream of his best friend and brother. That sound would haunt him for a long time to come. Sleep was futile. He needed to check on Landon.

Slipping into the room next door, he stopped and took in the scene before him. Landon was sleeping quietly, and Nova was curled up in a chair, pulled up next to his bed. Her throw had slipped to the floor, so Sawyer padded across the room, picked it up, and gently covered her. She smiled in her sleep and pulled the blanket up to her neck.

He couldn't stop staring at her. Nova was a beautiful woman, with waves of long silver-blue hair falling down to her waist. Like most shifter females, she was tall, with an athletic build, but still retained feminine curves he appreciated. Her eyes were blue, as light as a summer sky, filled with a keen intelligence and compassion. Best of all, she was his Fated Mate. His wolf couldn't understand why he was merely staring at her and not claiming her.

Sawyer shook his head in silent mirth. His wolf was in for a lesson in patience. This female was strong-willed and a definite alpha, so there would be no rushing her. To be honest, he was glad she was like that because he would need some time to work out not only the logistics, but how to share his life with another.

It had been only him and Landon for years now and they were settled in their lifestyle, always on the road, with no one to answer to. That would change now, and Sawyer wasn't sure how it would work out.

Nova stirred, slowly opening her eyes. She smiled at Sawyer, then looked over at Landon. Once she was satisfied her patient was still sleeping, she turned her attention back to Sawyer.

"Couldn't sleep?"

"Nah, kept hearing his scream in my dreams." Sawyer raked his trimmed beard. "Figured I'd come check on the two of you."

"If he reacts the same way as the other cases I've seen, he'll need a couple more injections before it starts flushing his system." Nova leaned forward and gently pulled back a corner of the bandage. "The streaks haven't progressed any further, so we have that going for us."

"Is there anything I can do to help?"

"I need the trap. I want to examine it and see how the silver was applied, plus my dad is going to want it for evidence. Hopefully, the storm will have moved on enough for my father's enforcers to come over in the morning so you can lead them back to search for it."

"I'm game. I just hope I can find the spot."

"I have faith in you." Nova tugged on his hand, giving it a squeeze.

"I'm glad you do, because my confidence has taken a blast these past few days. I knew better than to charge up this mountain, but I let Landon talk me into it." Sawyer sat on the foot of the bed, careful not to disturb his sleeping friend. "Same with the bear trap incident. I told Landon we needed to wait until morning, but he didn't listen. He was so focused on getting up here and finding something."

"Do you know what he was looking for?"

"Other than winter shots for a new portfolio, not really."

"Is he always like that?"

"Yes and no." Sawyer shrugged while he considered how to explain Landon's sixth sense. "He's always been focused on his passions, but it's more than that. He has a unique gift, I guess you could call it. Landon gets these *feelings* that always lead him to the best locations for his photos, the best place to stop and eat, things like that. It's gotten us out of jams more than once."

"Except this time," Nova noted.

Sawyer winced. "You're right. I didn't say it was flawless." He sighed heavily. "It was a complete misstep. He jumped to the side not to mess up a set of tracks and landed right on the damn thing."

This time, Nova winced.

"I heard him," she whispered. Her eyes widened at the memory. "I was getting more firewood for the night and heard a blood-curdling scream. I waited, but heard nothing else, finally dismissing it as the wind."

"That was Landon. He only screamed one time. I was right behind him when it happened and rushed to pry the trap open to get his leg out."

"You were wearing gloves. That's why you didn't know it was silver-laced," Nova pointed out.

"Yeah." Sawyer nodded in agreement. "There was so much blood... all I knew was I needed help, and fast. I used my belt as a tourniquet, slung him over my shoulder, and headed down the mountain. Fortunately, I saw smoke from your chimney and headed in your direction."

"He's lucky you were with him," Nova said softly.

"I'm lucky *you* were here," Sawyer corrected. "I would have lost him if you hadn't been."

"We're not out of the woods yet," Nova sighed. "He still has a long struggle ahead of him." Nova stood and stretched. "I could use some coffee. How about you?"

"Sounds great," Sawyer said with a smile. "I'd offer to make it, but I don't know where everything is."

"You can catch it next round." Nova laughed easily. "I need to stretch my legs anyway. Back in a bit."

Sawyer watched her leave, feeling a tinge of loss when the door closed behind her. *Did the mate bond work that fast? He hadn't claimed her. Was there even a bond yet?* All he knew was he wanted her back in the room with him, and his wolf was in total agreement.

Nova eased from the bedroom, making a beeline for the coffee maker. Once she got that under way, it was time to get the fire going again. Being a shifter, she always ran hot, but in Wyoming's harsh winters she needed the in-floor radiant heating to warm the cabin. Most of all, she loved her fireplace, even having one in her bedroom. She hadn't made it up the stairs last night, preferring to keep a close eye on her patient.

Thinking of Landon reminded her to call her father. He needed to know what was going on, and he wasn't going to be thrilled about silver bear traps on his mountain.

"What's wrong, sweetheart?"

"Good morning to you too, Dad. How is everyone?" Nova replied cheekily.

"I'm going to let that one slide because I know something is wrong. Out with it," he growled low into the phone.

Nova sighed. She'd never be able to get anything past him.

"I presently have two houseguests. Two men. One got caught in a bear trap, and the other one was carrying him down the mountain when they spotted smoke from my cabin."

"A bear trap! Fucking hunters... don't they know bears hibernate in the winter?"

"I don't think it was meant for bears, Dad. It was laced with silver. The men are shifters and I'm dealing with silver poisoning."

"Holy fuckin' crap! Does this get any worse? Who are they?"

"Sawyer Billings and Landon Monroe... they're not from the pack, and before you start, they weren't planning on being on the mountain more than an afternoon. That's why they didn't seek you out for permission," Nova hurried on, knowing her father's temper about trespassers. "The storm caught them unawares... let it slide, Dad." He was firm on his stand about people who didn't have the sense to be outdoors. "The injured man is a photographer, and he didn't see the trap buried in the snow."

"If I send Bryce and Linc out to your place, can your houseguest take them to the spot where the trap is?"

"He's willing to try. I've already told him that's what you would probably want to do."

"That's my girl. Let me get things rolling on this end. Expect company in about an hour."

Nova finished setting up a tray with coffee for two while she spoke to her dad... which went way better than she'd expected. Sawyer met her at the bedroom doorway, taking the tray from her.

"Thanks." She smiled up at him, enjoying the way his face lit up at such a simple thing. She was drawn to him, curious to know more about him, knowing it was the mate connection at work.

"I spoke to my dad. He's sending two of his best enforcers and trackers to help you find the trap. Bryce and Linc are cool. They won't give you a hard time."

"Have you taken to reading my mind now?" Sawyer blew on his coffee before taking a sip. "When you look at me, it's like you see the real me."

"Isn't that what Fated Mates are all about?" Nova asked curiously. She was definitely going to have a conversation with her mother in the very near future.

"I guess... hell, I have no idea. I've never known anyone who had a Fated Mate, much less discussed it with anyone, and I sure never expected to find my own." He gave her a sheepish grin. "All I know is when you look at me, you see the real me... and you don't look away."

"Who hurt you, Sawyer?" Nova set her coffee down and knelt beside him. "Who betrayed you so badly that you don't even know your own worth anymore?"

"Is it that obvious?" He swallowed hard, forcing himself to meet her eyes.

"It is to me." She laced her fingers with his and kissed his knuckles. "You're my mate, and the first rule is no secrets between us. Deal?"

"Deal!" Sawyer pulled Nova up between his legs, so she sat perched on his knee and wrapped his arms around her. "I promise to tell you my whole sordid past, but it's going to have to wait. I need to get dressed before your dad's men get here. They may be cool, but I bet they're not real patient."

Nova laughed, then kissed Sawyer softly on the lips.

"You have a point. We'll talk later. I'm going to give Landon another injection while you get dressed."

They both looked over at the injured man who was beginning to stir in his sleep.

"Timing is everything." Nova hurried to prepare the syringe before Landon came fully awake.

A sharp rap sounded from the front of the house.

"Damn, they had to be early," Nova muttered.

"I'll get it. You tend to Landon. Maybe I can talk them into some coffee while they wait."

"Good idea. I knew I made a full pot for a reason."

Once Sawyer left the room, Nova didn't waste a moment. She knew what was coming. With quick and precise movements, she injected the serum into Landon's vein, then peeled back the bandage on his leg. The black streaks hadn't progressed, but they hadn't lessened, either. The silver was still in his system, and his organs would start to shut down, one by one, if the antidote didn't start working.

As if on cue, Landon started retching and Nova grabbed the trash can. Poor guy had nothing on his stomach, so it was more of a painful dry heaving than anything else. When he finished, he limply fell back onto the bed, exhausted from his efforts. Nova grabbed wipes and towels and started cleaning him up.

"Hurts..." The groan was low and full of pain.

"I know, I'm trying to help, but you're in rough shape."

Long, dark lashes any female would die for, opened to dark brown eyes racked with pain.

"Who... who are you?"

"I'm Nova, and I'm taking care of you. Sawyer is here, so you're safe." She almost choked on an intake of air when he reached for her hand as she wiped his face. The current running through her at his touch was exactly the same as the contact between her and Sawyer.

What the hell?

A corner of Landon's mouth turned up slightly, and his eyes fluttered closed once again.

"There you are. I found you."

4

Nova's heart raced at Landon's words. *"There you are. I found you."* She remembered Sawyer saying that Landon had been focused on coming to the mountain and looking for something. Had he been looking for her? Had he known his Fated Mate lived on Bighorn? And to top it all off, she had not one, but *two* Fated Mates? *Was it even a thing?*

She desperately needed time to process, but now was not the time. She could hear Bryce's and Linc's low rumbles as they spoke to Sawyer and the approach of footsteps. Turning back to Landon, she was relieved to find him fast asleep. She finished cleaning him and changing his bandages as the door opened to the two enforcers.

"Morning, Nova."

"Hey, Bryce. Thanks for braving the weather so early in the morning." She looked over at Linc and grinned. "Appreciate you giving up your beauty sleep, big guy."

"Hmph," Linc grunted. "Only because it's you, so consider yourself fortunate."

"I do, big guy, every day." She winked at him, then laughed out loud when she saw his lips twitch into a surly smile.

"Sawyer's getting dressed, then we're headed up to where they camped." Bryce walked over to the side of Landon's bed and stared down at the injured man. "He gonna make it?" He asked in a low voice.

"I'm hoping." In that moment, Nova knew she would fight with every ounce of her being to save this male. If the Goddess meant for her to have two mates, she would accept them both with gratitude and figure out the details later.

A rustle of movement behind her pulled Nova from her thoughts. She hadn't realized she'd been standing in one spot, staring at Landon, until Sawyer walked up behind her.

"I'm headed out with the guys. Are you going to be okay with Landon?"

"Yeah." She cleared her throat. "Yeah, I'll be fine. I changed his bandages and gave him another injection. He should be good for a few hours."

"Oh, hell, I almost forgot. Be right back." Bryce said, then hurried from the room. Seconds later, he was back with an insulated bag.

"Your mom said to give this to you. It's got some meds you'd left there a while back. She said you might be able to use them."

"I love you, Mom," Nova breathed as she reached for the bag. Opening it, she found two bottles of morphine among other smaller vials of miscellaneous meds she used on dogs in her clinic, gauze, and bandages. Dinner with her parents one evening had ended up with her treating a neighbor's small dog, and she'd forgotten the bag in the refrigerator when she'd left. The Fates continued to line things up for her.

"Thanks, Bryce. This is going to help a lot." She turned to Sawyer. "Once the antitoxin starts flushing the silver from his system, he's going to be in a lot more pain." She held up the bottles. "This is going to help."

"Let's get a move on," Bryce said. "The sooner we get the trap, the better off we'll be."

Sawyer hugged Nova, and she didn't miss the raised brows of the enforcers, but they said nothing, and she knew they would keep it to themselves. Nova wasn't ready for explanations to anyone about having two Fated Mates. She had more important things on her mind right now.

Once the males left, Nova took the time to grab a bagel from the kitchen and nibble on it while she watched over Landon. If her calculations were right, the silver should start making its way out of Landon's system, and no matter how it happened, it would be messy and painful for the patient. Finishing off the bagel, she laid out the supplies she knew she would need—morphine, towels, and gauze for starters.

Silver in a shifter's system worked its way out in different ways. Sometimes the antidote forced the silver back into the open wound, which was better for the patient and easier to clean up. It was when it seeped through the pores that it got complicated. Silver burned like fire, and the patient would go through excruciating agony during the process.

Nova prayed Landon wouldn't have to deal with it, but looking at the streaks, she had her doubts. The silver had started to spread in the last hour, which wasn't a good sign. With everything laid out, she triple-gloved her hands and waited. She'd been burned by silver before, and it had been a kind of pain she didn't care to repeat.

Landon's agonized scream shattered the quiet and Nova whirled around to see what had happened. The male was tearing at his bandages, howling in pain. Rushing to his side, she scooped up the prepared syringe and injected the morphine into his thigh. It wasn't as good as directly into the vein, but he was moving around way too much for her to hit so small a target.

The silver was seeping through the wounds, and Landon had scratched at them, getting silver on his hands. With a determined effort, Nova began the battle to minimize the damage and save her mate's life.

"Fuck! It burns!"

"Landon! Listen to me. You need to stop thrashing around."

Even with her shifter strength, Nova was straining to keep the male still. Grabbing a roll of vet wrap, she snagged one of his wrists and bound him to the headboard. Rushing to the other side of the bed, she did the same with his other arm. The bed wouldn't hold up against a shifter in full panic mode, but she was out of options.

Wiping his hands clean of silver, she returned to his leg to find the silver seeping down his calf. Sitting astride his thighs, she was able to keep him from kicking out while she mopped up what she could of the mess. Silver was on the sheets, and he was lying in it, which didn't help the situation. With a crash, the bed gave way beneath them, and Nova rolled onto the floor with a groan.

"Make it stop! Sawyer! Make it fuckin' stop!"

Nova closed her eyes for a moment, wishing more than anything that Sawyer was here, at least to help hold the male down. She was having a devil of a time trying to contain the situation. Landon was a strong man, and right now, he had superpowers.

More than once, a drop or two of the liquid metal came into contact with her skin, leaving burns and singed flesh. She grimaced, but tending to her own wounds would have to wait. Landon's scream trailed off into whimpers of pain, and Nova breathed a small prayer to the Goddess. The morphine was kicking in at last.

Knowing she only had herself to depend on, Nova took a deep breath and went back to work. Taking advantage of the morphine respite, she continued to clean away the oozing silver while tearing the sheets out from under Landon's dead weight.

When the door opened, Bryce, Linc, and Sawyer found her sitting on the floor doctoring her burns while Landon lay on a mattress on the floor, headboard and footboard propped up against a wall.

"What the hell?" Linc growled.

"Don't ask," Nova said with an eye roll. "It got bad, and I had to deal with it."

"Nova, are you all right?" Sawyer knelt beside her, going over her burns and bruises.

He glanced over at his sleeping friend.

"Landon?"

Nova met his gaze, so full of worry and concern for both of them.

"The silver is working it's way out of the wound, which is better than oozing from his pores." She didn't miss the flinches from her dad's enforcers. They had seen enough to know the process was beyond painful.

"He was in acute distress, and I was forced to tie him down so I could tend to him. As you can see, it was a temporary fix." She noted Landon's even breathing and allowed herself to relax a tiny bit. "The first round of morphine I gave him was in the muscle because he was fighting so hard. Once it kicked in and

I was able to clean him and get everything under control, I gave him another injection directly into the vein. He should sleep for a few hours."

"Is it over then? Did all the silver come out?" Sawyer asked anxiously.

"I'm afraid not," Nova shook her head and pulled the sheet away from Landon's leg. Ugly gray and black streaks ran up his thigh and down to his ankle. "Those streaks are silver. That should give you an idea of what we're dealing with. We still have a long fight ahead of us." Nova turned to Bryce and Linc. "Did you find the trap?"

"Yeah," Bryce said. "Vile piece of work. Every tooth was dipped in silver."

"Never saw anything like it before," Linc added. "I don't know how it was done, but the silver is soft and there's a lot of it missing... like when the trap snapped around his leg, the silver melted into his skin."

"It would explain those streaks in his leg." Nova shuddered. "But I've never heard of silver doing that before. You think this is magical?"

"It would almost have to be," Bryce agreed. "It's some hellish work, regardless."

"We can take the snowmobiles into town if you need something from your clinic," Linc offered. "Make us a list, and we'll get it for you."

"You guys are angels." Nova blinked back the sting of tears. "That would be awesome. I've got a notepad in the kitchen. I won't be but a minute."

Hurrying to the kitchen, Nova grabbed the notepad and pen she kept on the counter for a running grocery list. Jotting down the items she'd need, she grabbed her keys on the way back to the bedroom. She came to a complete stop in the doorway to find Bryce, Linc, and Sawyer huddled around Landon.

"Did something happen? Is he all right?"

Sawyer met her gaze first.

"He's still sleeping." Sawyer glanced at the other two, then back to her. "We were trying to figure out a way to immobilize Landon without any further damage to him or your furniture."

Nova was touched by their concern. She wondered if the enforcers could somehow sense the two males were her Fated Mates but dismissed the thought as soon as it entered her mind. She hadn't been claimed by either of them, so there was no scent or mark to detect.

"That would be helpful because he's not out of the woods by a long shot," Nova admitted. "There's a massive amount of silver in his system and it needs to come out." She bit her lip as she cautiously glanced at Sawyer. She didn't want to freak him out, but he needed to be aware of the risks. "I'm going to increase the times I give him the antidote. If I don't see a marked improvement in the next twelve hours, I'm increasing the dosage."

"What kind of time frame are you giving him, Nova?" Sawyer asked quietly.

"If the silver remains, he might have three or four days."

She reached for Sawyer's hand, and he took it, pulling her into an embrace. His breathing was ragged against her ear, and she knew he was close to losing it. Then he kissed her lightly on the cheek and released her.

"Guess we have work to do."

5

Sawyer stayed behind in the bedroom with Landon while Nova walked the enforcers out, explaining her alarm system at the clinic. Pulling up a chair beside the bed, he stared at the younger man. They were raised as brothers and during the course of their lifetime became best friends. He didn't know how to deal without Landon in his life. He'd always been there for him, a ready ear to listen to his problems, the one to share jokes and secrets with. Somehow, some way, he needed to pull through this crisis.

He knew in his heart Nova was doing all she could. Surprisingly, even the enforcers had gone out of their way to help by offering to go into town to retrieve the medicine and supplies Nova needed to help his brother. In the end, though, it was up to Landon.

The kid had a rough beginning, and life hadn't been kind to him. Sawyer had taken it upon himself to champion the young pup from the get-go, from getting into fights with bullies who picked on the abandoned child to taking the blame for the scrapes Landon managed to land in, time after time. He'd do it all over again. The male was his brother in every way but blood.

Sawyer caught a whiff of honeysuckle, triggering memories of lazy summer days and happier moments, and realized the scent came from Nova. His wolf chuffed happily, and he couldn't say it didn't make him feel a little better, too.

Nova rested her hands on his shoulders, lightly massaging the tense muscles. He groaned in appreciation of her skilled touch.

"Like that?" There was a hint of laughter in her question.

"Who wouldn't?" Sawyer sighed happily. "You have amazing hands."

"You haven't seen anything yet." Laughter poured from Nova, and it was the sweetest sound he'd heard in ages.

Standing, Sawyer captured her hands and pulled her in for an embrace, then kissed her unhurriedly, learning what she responded to the most, making sure he repeated it. When he pulled away, his head swam with new and exciting emotions. Nova was his

Fated Mate, and they were meant to be together. He'd figure out the rest later.

"Going by your talented hands and that kiss, I'd say my future looks amazingly bright."

Nova didn't act coy. She met his gaze full on, her smile sensual and filled with satisfaction. Damned if he didn't like that—a lot.

"I'm reasonably sure if the Goddess puts people together, she's not going to mess up the outcome."

"I like that." Sawyer gently caressed her cheek and thrilled at the way she leaned into his touch. "I'm going to remember that when things get rough." He couldn't help but glance at Landon in the bed beside them.

"I have a feeling things are going to work out, but we'll have to do our part to make it happen."

Sawyer met her gaze and wondered, not for the first time, who this alluring and enigmatic female truly was. Nova was the epitome of all things he found attractive and desirable in a female but never hoped to find in his lifetime. What had changed in his life to be given such a precious gift? Why now, after all this time? Figuring it was best not to question the Goddess or the Fates, he would accept it gratefully and humbly and do his best to be worthy of such a treasure.

"It burns! Sawyer, help me!" Landon cried out.

Turning to him as one, Nova and Sawyer went to each side of the bed. Already drenched in sweat, Landon tossed and turned, fighting the restraints holding him in place, his face etched in pain. Sawyer grabbed towels from a pile on the nightstand and began wiping the male down, trying to comfort him in a low voice while giving Nova time to prepare the syringes needed for the injections.

"Nova? Is that silver?" Sawyer's shock promptly turned to horror as he saw the deadly liquid metal oozing from his brother's pores.

"Yes! Put some gloves on, quick! Two or three pair if you can get them on. You don't want it to burn you." Nova handed a bucket to Sawyer over the bed. "Swipe the silver off his skin with the gauze and throw it in here." She wiped her brow with her sleeve. "This isn't how I would've wanted it to happen, but at least the silver is starting to find its way out, and that's a good sign."

She looked him dead in the eye while saying those last words and Sawyer took it for gospel. It's what they needed to happen for Landon to survive.

The next minutes… hours… Sawyer lost track of time, were spent cleaning oozing silver from Landon's body. Every spot it touched left a red and raw burn. Luckily, if there were such a thing in a situation like this, the silver was centralized in Landon's legs, though even Sawyer, without any medical training, knew the silver was in his blood system throughout his body.

"Hey, Nova! We're back," Bryce called from the doorway. "You need any of that stuff right now?"

"Yes, please. I need the gauze. We've got a mess over here."

Without another word, the enforcers left and returned laden with medical supplies. By the looks of it, they had everything Nova had asked for and extra.

"Old man Dickerson had the store open and running it by himself, stubborn ole fool. We took advantage of it and cleaned out his medical section and bought more groceries." Linc gave her a wink and a toothy grin. "Knew you would be stocked up, but you weren't expecting company. Figured a few extra steaks and potatoes wouldn't hurt."

"You guys are lifesavers. Leave me a total so I can square up with you."

"I'm gonna act like I didn't hear that." Bryce looked offended.

"Guys..."

"Not another word, Nova Adkins." Linc raised a hand to halt any protest. "Your dad is our Alpha, and you're like a sister to us. We're pack... you know we take care of each other."

Nova smiled up at the two burly males.

"Thank you. Your generosity is very much appreciated."

"That's better—" Bryce said smugly. "If there's nothing else, we need to head back. The weather is kicking back up again. I think we hit the lull just right."

"Get back while you can and be careful. Thanks for everything."

After the enforcers had closed the door behind them, Sawyer glanced at Nova.

"It's always like that?"

"With Bryce and Linc? Or the whole pack?"

"Both, I guess—" Sawyer said haltingly.

"I'm especially close to Bryce and Linc." She hurried on to qualify her statement. "Like they said, being Dad's enforcers, they're like brothers to me and my sisters, but the whole pack is like that. We're a close-knit unit. My dad is a good Alpha, and he's respected on the mountain."

"You're very fortunate."

"I am, and I'm aware of it too. I don't take any one of them for granted." Nova stretched her back, then peeled off her gloves, dropping them into the bucket holding the silver-tainted gauze.

"That's all we can do for now." Nova gave him a weak smile. "He's got enough drugs in him to knock out a small elephant for a day. I'm hoping he manages a few hours of rest."

By the time they'd cleaned the injured male and changed his bedding, Sawyer felt like he'd been through a tortuous workout and Nova wasn't faring much better.

"Nova, you need to sleep. Why don't you grab a shower and get some rest?" Sawyer was quick to recognize the stubbornness in the female's eyes when someone told her what to do. She wasn't one to be pushed around and he respected her for it, but right now, she needed someone to take care of her, and that's where he came in.

"You've been going non-stop since we got here, and that's not good for you. I promise to come and get you if Landon needs help, but you need sleep... in your bed, not in the next room, listening and waiting."

Nova started to say something, then caught herself. She shook her head and gave him a crooked smile.

"You're right. I could use some rest."

Sawyer could see the weariness in her eyes and pressed his lips to hers softly.

"Feel free to dig around in the kitchen for something to eat."

"Stop taking care of us for a minute." He raised a brow and shook his head. "Think about yourself." He gently pushed her in the direction of the stairs. "Believe me, if my brother were in better shape, I'd be the one taking care of you. I'd like to think you'd enjoy my brand of pampering."

"We'll get there." She gave him a wink and softly padded up the stairs.

More tired than she would ever admit and still she kept giving. Sawyer thought his heart would burst from the happiness swelling inside.

Nova slid beneath the bubbles and hot water, moaning in a mixture of relief and pleasure. The water felt so good on her sore and aching body, but she would have to be careful not to fall asleep right where she was.

She was exhausted, and she hated that Sawyer had called her on it, but the male wasn't stupid... not by a long shot. He was learning her as quickly as she was learning him. There were so many facets to Sawyer, and she was intrigued with every one of them she discovered. He'd promised to tell her about his past. They had plenty of time to get to know one another, but that was the story she wanted to know about the most.

Someone in his past had hurt Sawyer, not a broken-heart kind of pain, but a deep-down betrayal that shook him to his foundation, where he doubted his own worth as a male. Nova needed to know more, so she could help him heal. Sawyer was an alpha in his own right, but he didn't exude confidence like every other alpha she'd met. She couldn't begin to imagine what had happened to strip the basic fiber of his being.

Then there was Landon, her other Fated Mate, the one she knew nothing about, except what Sawyer had told her. She hadn't yet told Sawyer about Landon also being her mate, or about what he'd said to her. Almost every waking second had been spent tending to Landon's injuries, and finding a moment to tell your new Fated Mate that his brother was in the equation of Fated Mates was not something Nova was ready to deal with. She could barely deal with the idea of having one mate, much less two!

Nova rose from the rapidly cooling water and toweled off. Slipping on thick pajama bottoms and a t-shirt, she eased into bed. She didn't remember anything after that, falling into a deep, dreamless sleep.

6

"Nova... Nova!"

She heard Sawyer's voice calling her, but it came from far away. Her head felt heavy, and her thoughts were muddled. All she wanted was a few more minutes of sleep. *Was that too much to ask?*

"Nova!"

Filled with urgency, that last call got her attention, and she sat up instantly, scanning the room. Sawyer stood at the foot of her bed, wearing a pair of sweats and nothing else. Her mind registered the chiseled six-pack and light dusting of chest hair, appreciating the narrow trail leading beneath the sweats, riding low on his hips.

"I need your help. Landon's awake, and he's in a lot of pain."

"I'm coming." Throwing back the covers, Nova jumped out of bed and headed for the door. Lustful thoughts of Sawyer were put on the back burner once again. Sprinting down the stairs with Sawyer fast on her heels, she didn't waste time, going straight for the meds.

"What time is it?" Nova was still shaking off the drowsiness clouding her thoughts, needing to know how long it had been since Landon's last injection.

"It's eight in the evening. The two of you have been out for six hours." Sawyer nodded toward a thermos on the side table. "I made coffee an hour ago and fixed a thermos for you. Figured it was getting close to Landon waking, and you might appreciate a cup or two."

"You're a gem." Nova smiled at Sawyer as she gave Landon the injections that would ease his pain and force the silver from his system.

Sawyer was already at work, wiping the silver away as it forced its way out of Landon's body. They worked together in tandem, swiftly and efficiently, and before she knew it, Sawyer was tossing out the tainted gauze and she was putting away her equipment.

"I found something in one of the boxes the guys brought back with them. It might come in handy," Sawyer mentioned as he set out fresh gauze and towels.

Turning back to him, she raised a quizzical brow.

"What did I miss?"

"This." He held up two small devices, slightly smaller than her cell phone. "It's a baby monitor. We leave this one in here, and take this one with us in another room, like the kitchen. We can hear when Landon starts to stir." He shrugged as he gave them to her. "I know we'd probably hear him regardless, but it's a backup. I figured it might be useful."

"It's a good idea. I'll have to thank Bryce and Linc for thinking of it." She studied the devices carefully. "I have to admit, it would give us a little more freedom to move around."

"That's what I was thinking." He took the portable monitor from her. "I'm going to fix us something to eat, and I'd like you to join me."

"Sounds wonderful." She smiled up at him. "Let me plug this in and make sure Landon is settled. I'll be there in a few minutes."

Gazing down at Landon, she couldn't resist the urge to push back a lock of dark brown hair from his forehead. He was sleeping peacefully until she touched him.

"Nova?"

"Yes, it's me. I'm sorry I disturbed you. Go back to sleep. You need the rest."

He reached for her hand, and she gave it, sitting next to him on the bed.

"Needed to make sure you were real," he mumbled. "Keep dreaming of searching for you."

"You found me, and I'm very much real."

"It's true, then? We're Fated Mates?"

"It is... Sawyer, too."

He'd closed his eyes, but they opened again at her words.

"The three of us are mates? Sweet. I'm gonna rest now."

Nova chuckled lightly and brushed her lips against his forehead, grateful to notice he wasn't running a fever.

"Rest now."

Nova plugged in the monitor, did a sound check with Sawyer, then headed for the kitchen. She couldn't put it off any longer. She had to tell Sawyer about Landon.

Sawyer tasted the chili and smiled, setting the spoon down on the stove. It was one of the few recipes he got from his mom that even he couldn't mess up. He smiled even more when Nova's arms wrapped around his waist.

"Something sure smells good in here," she purred.

He turned in her arms and kissed her soundly.

"I'd like to think it was me, but I'm fairly sure the chili is going to win this one," he husked against her ear.

"The chili *does* smell good, but I'm perfectly content where I am."

"I'll call that a win." He winked at her with a smirk. "Let's grab some bowls. I've worked up an appetite."

Reaching into the oven, he pulled out two muffin pans.

"What are those?" Nova's eyes widened.

"Sweet cornbread muffins. Nothing goes better with chili. I'll stake my reputation on it."

"Mmm, sounds wonderful."

It didn't take long before they were settled at the table with big bowls of chili and cornbread muffins. He liked the way Nova dug into her food with relish. Nothing shy about that one.

"I know the food has got your attention, but you're awfully quiet. Is everything all right?" He asked cautiously.

Nova wiped her mouth with a napkin and dropped it beside her plate.

"I need to tell you something, and I'm not sure how you're going to handle it."

"With a lead-in like that, I need fortification." Sawyer pushed his bowl away and took a long swig of his beer.

"Yesterday, when I was tending to Landon while you were letting in Bryce and Linc, he woke briefly. I was wiping his face, and he caught my hand. The same exact feeling I had when you and I touched happened between Landon and me." She searched his face before she finished. "He said, 'There you are. I found you,' then he fell asleep."

"Can't say I saw that coming."

"There's more." She proceeded to tell him what had transpired in the bedroom a few minutes before. "I've heard of Fated Mates and heard a lot about mixed shifter relationships, but having two Fated

Mates is new to me." She held up her hands helplessly. "Is it even a thing?"

"It's a thing." Sawyer's mind raced, trying to dredge up every bit of information he'd ever heard about multiple mates. "I'm not sure about the numbers, so I'm going to hazard a guess and say it's rare, but I've heard about females having multiple mates, as many as four or five."

"Fated Mates?" Nova squeaked.

"Yeah, and it works for them." Sawyer stood and reached for Nova's hand. "Let's go sit on the sofa where we can be more comfortable."

Leading her to the living room, he made sure she sat next to him so he could touch her. He needed her touch more than ever right now. This whole Fated Mate thing was new to him. He hadn't even claimed her yet, and now, he had to share her... with his brother?

Nova's gentle hands cupped his face as she gazed into his eyes.

"I take it you aren't as accepting as Landon?"

"It's not that... shit, maybe it is. It's all new. I haven't claimed you yet, and now I have to share you with my brother. I simply don't know how it's all going to work." He was so relieved when Nova pulled him into her arms. He was being petty and more than a little jealous, but he couldn't help it. He'd shared everything with Landon his whole life... now he had to share his mate? It wasn't fair!

"Sawyer, listen to me. I don't know how it's going to work, either, but we're a unit now and we'll figure it out... together."

Then she kissed him, and every petty thought, every doubt and worry, flew from his mind when her scent enveloped him, and her ripe lips worked their magic. The sharp need of her kiss set his soul on fire, and the alpha in him, battered and long buried, rose to the surface to claim their mate. Nova's kisses were wild with passion, brazen kisses holding nothing back.

"If you don't stop this now, I'm going to claim you right here on the sofa," he growled low.

"Just so there's no confusion, I'm not stopping, and the sofa is fine."

Nova sat back, tearing off her clothes in a rush, then looked back at him, lust and heat in her eyes. She exuded the alpha female, confident in herself and knowing what she wanted.

Sawyer watched her in awe, dumbstruck by her beauty and grace. She was everything he never knew he wanted, and if he had to share her with Landon, so be it, but by the Goddess, he would claim his mate first.

Following suit, he discarded his clothes, then pulled Nova down on top of him. Spiking his fingers in her long hair, he cradled her head and kissed her long and deep, his tongue dancing with hers, as he held her tightly along his length. She ground against him, working his shaft into hardened steel so hard it hurt, but he didn't try to enter her.

He needed to discover his mate, find out where she was most sensitive, what she liked most, and he did, taking his time with kisses, caresses, nips, and touch.

The air was filled with her arousal, and when Nova impaled herself on his shaft, she cried out his name. She was deliciously tight as she whimpered against him. He stilled, not wanting to hurt her, waiting for her to make the next move when she was ready. After a moment or two, she lifted her hips, then lowered, meeting his strokes, thrust for thrust. Her heat melted around his cock and Sawyer could only guide as Nova took over, satisfying herself, which in turn, was the hottest thing he'd ever seen.

When she collapsed against his chest, he rolled them over, ramming himself home, his body hard and filled with a primal need to fill her and claim her as his. Hard, rough strokes rocked her body, and her cries of passion were an ancient song of love and lust.

The need to explode built higher, and he was desperate to climax. In a quick movement, he turned Nova onto her knees, slamming into her from behind. His balls tightened, and he growled with pleasure. No woman had ever felt so good, so perfect, so meant to be his. With a shout, he spilled deep inside her, his canines lengthening and striking their mark in the junction of her shoulder, claiming her as his Fated Mate.

Sawyer wanted to howl his joy alongside his wolf, but instead, he curled around Nova's length and held her tight, running his tongue over the claiming mark.

It would heal but she would always bear his mark, letting every male know she was his and protected.

They lay together as the mate bond worked its magic, letting the other into their thoughts and feelings. Nova was already falling in love with him, and it would continue to grow stronger with time. She had feelings for Landon but didn't know him yet. Nova was patient. She would take her time with her other mate, but now, her entire focus was on Sawyer and pleasing him. Nothing could have made him happier.

"I love you, Nova, and I will spend my life showing you exactly how much."

7

Nova burrowed against Sawyer, happy and satiated, letting the mate bond work its magic between them. She had no regrets about letting Sawyer claim her first, she had too many questions about having two mates and wanted to slow-walk dealing with both males at the same time. The fact that Landon was injured made it an easy decision.

"How about we take this upstairs to my bed?" Nova asked in a breathy whisper. "We'd be a lot more comfortable."

Sawyer held her even tighter and gently bit the lobe of her ear.

"I'm doing fine right here, but it would make more sense. Besides, I'll have more room to explore." His chuckle was low and gravelly against her ear.

Getting up from the couch, Nova snagged the monitor, then returned to Sawyer with a wink.

"Race you!" She couldn't help but laugh as Sawyer caught her halfway up the stairs, scooped her up, and tossed her onto the bed. "If I'd known you were that fast, I would've given myself a better head start."

"Never underestimate a male who just sampled the best sex of his life," he growled. "I definitely want more."

"I like where this is going," Nova purred. "But before we go there..." She laughed as his face fell. "I want to talk first. You promised to tell me about yourself, and I want to hear your story." She bit his bottom lip, then sucked it sensually. "Then, we'll play."

"You don't play fair, but a deal is a deal." Sawyer groaned but managed to control himself.

"I knew you were a male of your word." Nova grinned triumphantly. "Now spill. I want to help you, but I have to understand first."

"Darling, I appreciate your intent, but I don't think even you can help fix me. I'm broken."

She shivered in delight when he called her *darling.* She'd never been one for pet names but had a feeling she wouldn't get tired of this one. Go figure. This mate thing was already changing how she felt and thought about things.

"Why don't you tell me, and I'll be the judge of whether or not I can help."

"Only if you let me hold you while I do it."

Nova pulled back the comforter, and they lay beneath the sheets, Sawyer holding her tucked against his side. Drawing circles on his chest with a finger, she looked up at him.

"Now?"

"You *are* persistent," Sawyer muttered.

"You have no idea how persistent I can be." She chuckled wickedly.

"I was afraid of that." He rolled his eyes. "But a deal is a deal, so here goes. When I was in my teens, there was a female..."

"Wait, I've heard that one before." Nova giggled.

"Probably not this version." He brought her hand to his lips and sensually sucked her index finger. "Any more interruptions and we make love instead."

Nova's intake of air was audible.

"Umm, okay... no more interruptions... for now."

This time, it was Sawyer's turn to chuckle.

"As I was saying, her name was Catrina, and she was the most beautiful female in the pack. I was elated when she chose me to be her first. We ended up inseparable for the better part of a year. I knew we weren't Fated Mates, but my parents weren't either, and they made it work. I was already thinking of settling down with her and raising pups."

"My pack was a motorcycle club, and I worked in the garage after school, maintaining their bikes. It kept me in enough pocket money to take Cat to the movies on the weekend and eat out now and then, plus I was learning a trade. I thought I had it made until one night a group of older kids caught me unawares while I was headed home. They dragged me out to the woods and beat the living crap out of me. The leader, Jed Price, told me he'd had enough of watching me fuck his girl, and he was putting a stop to it."

Sawyer took a deep breath, and the exhale came out shaky. Nova knew he was reliving it as he told her because the anguish was so obvious on his face. She held him tighter, trying to comfort him, but she knew he had to get it out. Sawyer could only vanquish his demon by facing it.

"That was the night it all came out. It turned out I wasn't Cat's first. I was a bet, one she'd taken full advantage of. In fact, she was there when they beat me, laughing and calling me all sorts of vile names. Jed, who was the Alpha's son, told me I was worthless and would never amount to crap... his friends and Cat goaded him the whole time. The beatings and taunts continued until they eventually left me for dead in the woods."

"When I came to, I barely managed to drag myself home and tell my parents what had happened. My dad went to the Alpha to file a complaint, and they sent enforcers after me to face him. One look in his eyes and I knew he was aware of everything that had happened. I was pronounced unfit to be an alpha and stripped down to omega status."

"No Alpha can do that!" Nova gasped.

"I was a kid. What did I know? My dad wasn't about to say anything. Who knew what Price would've done to my parents and brother?"

Nova sat up, outraged and shaken by his story. Seeing the tears brimming in Sawyer's eyes, her heart broke for him.

"I'm so sorry I made you go through that," Nova whispered.

Sawyer pulled her back down into his arms and kissed her temple.

"You needed to know. I haven't spoken of it since that day, just kept it all inside."

"What happened to you afterward?"

"A couple of days later, when I was able to move around, I stuffed a backpack and a duffle bag with the few things I owned and set to leave. I had saved a little, enough for a bus ticket and to get by until I could find a job." He laughed low and bitterly. "Landon pitched a fit, not wanting me to go. He was six. I damn sure couldn't take him with me, so I made him a promise. When he turned eighteen, I would come back for him. I made him swear to finish school and not give our parents any crap. He agreed, and I left that day."

"You kept your word, didn't you?"

"Sure as fuck did," Sawyer growled low, his eyes glowing gold. "I was twenty-eight when I went back. I had worked my way through college, got a degree, and knew I could financially take care of my brother. I visited with Mom and Dad for a couple of hours while Landon packed. They understood the situation and weren't going to try to stop either one of us. I promised to keep in touch, and we've been on the road ever since."

"I'm so sorry I made you relive that nightmare. I promise never to bring it up again." Nova wiped away her tears. His story had been painful to hear. She couldn't imagine what he'd suffered growing up in a pack like that.

"It's taken its toll on me. For almost ten years now, Landon and I have been packless. It was my choice, but I never meant to put my brother through that kind of life."

"I don't know Landon yet, but I have a feeling he doesn't see it the same way you do," Nova said thoughtfully.

"He says it doesn't bother him, but it's not fair to him, either. He should be with a pack. Landon is a decent male and a damn good beta. He'd be better off with his own kind."

"Sawyer." Nova waited for his gaze to meet hers. "He *is* with his own kind." She rubbed his arm, hoping her touch would comfort him in some small way.

Sawyer relaxed under Nova's soft touch, and his thoughts circled back to what she'd said earlier about wanting to help him. Now, Sawyer was convinced that if it could happen, she would be the one to do it. Nova's love was bringing him back to life in ways he'd never imagined.

Hope flared inside him. Maybe this *could* work out after all. It would take time, and they still had to deal with Landon's healing, but there was a small beacon of light at the end of a very long tunnel, and Sawyer was going for it. It was worth the chance.

"Enough about me," Sawyer said as he pulled Nova into his arms. "A deal is a deal, and I told you about me. Now I want to know more about you." He nuzzled her neck and Nova giggled.

"You already know about me," she protested laughingly.

"Believe me, I haven't begun to know you." He knew his eyes flared gold when Nova looked back at him with heat in her gaze. He pushed her onto the mattress and covered her with his length, planting kisses everywhere he could reach.

It wasn't long before her giggles and smothered laughter turned to moans of pleasure, and Sawyer smiled to himself. He was gentle and tender with her, then with the nuance of a breath, he knew when she wanted more... never rough, but aggressive enough to make her cry out, wanting more.

Like everything else about her, Nova wasn't shy or coy. She knew what she wanted, what pleased her, and how to ask for it without being demanding. She was the epitome of the perfect partner and Sawyer's love for her was already growing stronger and deeper. He was beginning to feel like the male he should have been all along.

8

"Nova! Sawyer! Where are you guys?"

The voice was scared and sounded far away. Nova blinked, struggling to wake up.

"Guys! I could use some help."

"Crap! That's Landon." Sawyer sat up abruptly, jarring Nova fully awake.

Grabbing a t-shirt and yoga pants from a dresser drawer, Nova sprinted down the stairs right after Sawyer. They flew into the bedroom to find Landon tearing into a box of gauze on the bedside table. Evidence of his attempts to wipe away the oozing silver was scattered on the sheets and floor.

"Sorry about the mess, but this crap burns like hell," Landon rasped, his face bathed in sweat.

Nova and Sawyer wasted no time putting on gloves and helping to clean up the mess. Sawyer grabbed the bucket and began picking up the pieces of gauze while Nova worked on Landon's leg.

"I'll give you something for pain in a minute. Let me get this cleaned up first." Nova smiled at him. "I didn't expect to find you awake, much less tackling your own wound care."

"I haven't been awake very long, but I do feel a little better... or I did until that stuff started oozing out of my leg. What is it?" He stared at his fingers, the tips already raw with burns.

Sawyer tossed him some wipes.

"It's silver. Get it off your fingers with those."

"Silver? Where did that come from?" His shocked stare swung from one to the other. "The last thing I remember was trying not to mess up a set of tracks and something locking onto my leg."

"You stepped into a bear trap," Sawyer explained. "One coated in silver."

"We're thinking magic was involved," Nova added. "When the teeth bit into your leg, the silver dissolved into your bloodstream. We've been battling the poison in your system for a few days now. It's been a race to get it all out before your organs shut down."

Nova swiped at the wound one last time, waiting to see if more silver would come. After a few minutes, her brow rose in surprise.

"I hate to say anything too soon, but I think that was the last of the silver."

Sawyer's expression was filled with relief as he sat at the foot of the bed, peeling off his gloves.

"It was that bad?" Landon asked, watching Sawyer carefully.

"Yeah, bro. I almost lost you." Sawyer's voice was gruff with emotion. "I would have, too, if it hadn't been for Nova."

Landon turned to face Nova, his dark brown eyes filled with emotion.

"Thank you doesn't begin to cover it..."

Nova sat down beside Landon and kissed him softly on his lips.

"No thanks are needed."

Landon tensed for a moment, then pulled Nova against his chest, deepening the kiss. When he pulled back, he let out a ragged breath.

"Whoa, umm, I'm sorry?" He shook his head, then ran his fingers through his short hair. "Oh, hell... I'm not sorry about that at all." He glanced at Sawyer, who was watching them intently. "I didn't dream it, did I?"

Nova captured his hands and squeezed them gently.

"Nope, apparently, you were searching for Nova when we started this trip," Sawyer replied.

"And you found her..." Landon finished.

"In a roundabout way, circumstances brought us here."

"Turns out the three of us are Fated Mates," Nova said softly. She laughed lightly at the stunned look on Landon's face. "You woke once when I was tending to you and said, *There you are. I found you.*"

"I remember... I knew I was searching for something, but I had no idea what or who it was." Landon inhaled deeply, then tugged at the neckline of Nova's t-shirt. "You've been marked." He turned to Sawyer. "Yours?"

"Yeah, we didn't plan it. It just happened. We were both on shaky ground with the multiple mate thing and neither of us were sure about claiming."

"I get it. I'd kind of like to get to know Nova before claiming her." He grinned sheepishly at Nova. "If that's all right with you."

She smiled. Landon was charming and sensitive to her feelings. His beta was synced to Sawyer's alpha, and it explained a lot as to why they were so close.

"I feel the same way. Sawyer and I agreed to go slow, too, but the mate connection tends to amp things up." She shrugged helplessly.

"I don't mean to come off sounding lame, but how is this supposed to work?" Landon asked.

"Tell you what..." Sawyer stretched. "I need to stock up on firewood before it gets much later. How about the two of you get to know each other while waiting for Landon's drugs to kick in?"

Nova gave Sawyer a slight nod. She appreciated him for taking a step back to give Landon some privacy with her. There would be a lot of give and take in their future, and she was relieved to discover her mates were willing to do their part.

"Thanks." She walked over to Sawyer and kissed him tenderly. "I could use another bowl of chili if there's any left."

"I made enough for an army of wolves. I'll heat it up when I get back in."

"Chili?" Landon groaned.

"Not yet." Sawyer and Nova said simultaneously, then broke into laughter.

"You guys ain't right."

"It simply means you have to finish healing," Sawyer said with a grin as he walked from the room.

"He always knows best," Landon said with a long-suffering sigh.

"And you thought that would change?" Nova grinned. She returned to sit beside Landon on the bed. "I'm keeping you on the antitoxin and morphine until you can shift. When you can do that, I'll know all the silver is out of your system. In the meantime, you'll sleep." Before he could protest, she placed a finger against his lips. "Your body has been through hell and back, Landon. You must regain your strength. Sleep is what you need until your wolf can take over."

"You're the doc." He glanced up at her. "You *are* a doctor, right?"

Nova laughed out loud, and it felt good, pushing all the worry and tension away.

"Actually, I'm a veterinarian, but since half of you is wolf, it counts, right?"

"Yeah, I guess it does." Landon grinned.

☽●☾

Sawyer filled the log tote and headed back to the house. He'd already made one trip and figured this would hold them through the night, if not, he'd come and get more. Nova had a good stockpile of firewood that probably would last her for a couple of months, barring any more blizzards like the one they were dealing with.

He looked around but could only see darkness and a blanket of white. Everything was covered in snow, and it was falling hard and steady. The wind howled through the trees, driving the cold through any crack or crevice it could find. Whoever built Nova's cabin had done an excellent job because once inside, you never heard the wind.

Once the firewood was stacked neatly by the fireplace, Sawyer stoked the logs until flames danced and the wood crackled. Moving the screen in place, he knelt before the fire, watching the flames for a moment, lost in thought.

He hadn't been jealous or upset when Landon kissed Nova, which, to be honest, had surprised him. He'd expected it, was waiting for it. Instead, a sense of acceptance and completeness filled him. They were Nova's mates, and the three of them belonged together. It felt right.

Sawyer stood and stretched, then headed to the kitchen to heat the chili for their meal. He chuckled lightly when he thought of Landon's expression when he learned he would be missing out on the chili… it was one of his brother's favorites. He'd have to make another batch when Landon was doing better to make up for today.

Soft, supple arms snaked around him from behind and his wolf chuffed happily. *Mate*.

"Landon says you owe him big time."

"Still peeved about the chili?" Sawyer laughed. He turned to face Nova, holding her close. "I was planning on making more when he was better."

"You might want to start on that sooner rather than later. I won't be surprised if we find a wolf in his room come morning," she said with satisfaction.

"He's over it? The silver is all gone?" Sawyer could hardly believe what he was hearing. It was all he wanted... had prayed for... but to know Landon would be all right... it was nothing short of a miracle.

"I think I can safely say the silver is out of his system. The streaks are all gone, and I haven't seen any sign of oozing since we cleaned him. He's sleeping now and should for a few hours."

Sawyer pinched the bridge of his nose and blinked back the burn of tears. He'd almost lost his brother. It was only because of the woman before him that Landon was still here.

"I'll never be able to thank you enough for taking us in the other night... and saving him," Sawyer said gruffly.

"It was meant to be," Nova said softly. "Don't you know that by now?"

"I'm still trying to wrap my head around it." He kissed her lightly on the temple. "It's a lot to take in.

What went from the worst night of my life to the best thing that could've happened is a big stretch, especially from my standpoint. I haven't had that many highs in my life. Can you blame me?"

Nova molded her body against his, pressing him against the counter, which started up another set of emotions and urges flaring. He inhaled her scent, which grounded him in a way that was new to him. Being with her not only felt right but also natural and comfortable. Yes, it was where he was supposed to be.

"Whatever the reason, we've been blessed with our Fated Mates. I want you to try to put your past behind you and look to your future... one with Landon and me. We have a new life together, the three of us, and I look forward to sharing that life with the two of you."

She cupped his growing erection through his sweats, growling low in his ear.

"Seems I've woken the beast. Should we tend to him?"

"Most definitely. He's very high maintenance and requires a great deal of attention." Sawyer smirked.

"Let's not keep him waiting." Nova turned off the burner on the stove and swiped the monitor from the counter.

She didn't need to tell him twice. Sawyer was totally on board with whatever she had in mind. Scooping her into his arms, he headed for the stairs. When she pulled him in for a kiss, he groaned into her mouth. She tasted sweet, like ripe berries fresh off the vine. He couldn't wait to taste her other riches and hurried to the bedroom upstairs.

They spent the night exploring each other's bodies and desires, the thought of chili long forgotten and growing cold on the stove. There were other ways to sustain themselves and Sawyer had all he could ever dream of.

9

Nova woke reluctantly, wrapped in Sawyer's arms. She tried to move closer to snuggle against him, but a furry bulk lay between them. Giggling, she buried her fingers into Landon's rich coat and was rewarded with a lick on her cheek.

"I had a feeling you'd be shifting soon. You must be feeling better," she whispered.

The wolf chuffed, resting his head between his paws.

Nova teased Sawyer's lips with a kiss, keeping a hand buried in Landon's fur. He made no move to shift, lying quietly between them.

"Morning," Sawyer mumbled drowsily. "Did you sleep well?"

"I did, and I'm not the only one." Nova grinned as she waited for Sawyer to notice they weren't alone.

Sawyer's eyes opened wide as he took in the extra body in the bed.

"I see a bigger bed in our immediate future," Sawyer grumbled.

Landon made a sound somewhere between a chuff and a snort.

"Did he just laugh?" Nova asked.

"Give me grief, and you'll be on the floor in a heartbeat," Sawyer threatened.

Landon whined and covered his nose with a paw.

"You hurt his feelings," Nova fussed.

Sawyer sat up, stared at Nova in disbelief, then glared at his brother.

Landon shifted to his human form and held his hand up in surrender.

"I was only messing around, Sawyer. I didn't mean anything by it."

"What am I missing?" Nova asked.

"Landon has a habit of playing the 'charming card' with the ladies." Sawyer huffed in exasperation. "It's a game with him, and he knows I don't care for it. I'm not going to put up with that kind of crap between us. This is not a competition. We're Fated Mates."

"He's right," Landon said, eyes downcast. "I'm sorry, and I promise it won't happen again."

Nova reached for each of their hands and held them tightly.

"Sawyer's right on this one. I don't want you thinking you have to compete for my affection, and I don't ever want to take sides. I want to get past this right now and know for sure it won't ever happen again." She tugged Landon's hand until he met her gaze.

"I promise."

Nova crawled over to Landon and kneeling in front of him, she framed his face with her hands and teased his lips with a kiss that began softly, then built in intensity. When he reached for her, she pulled back.

"Not yet," she said softly. "You're not at full strength, and we need to get to know each other better before anything else happens." She stared deep into his brown eyes, wanting him to understand she wasn't playing favorites, but she wanted her feelings to be respectfully considered. "I want to make love to Sawyer right now. You're welcome to stay with us if you want. You can touch me, and kiss me, but that's as far as it will go today. This isn't a punishment. I need you to understand, Landon."

"I get it." He glanced over at Sawyer. "If it's all right with you, I'd like to stay with the two of you."

Sawyer's eyes were a brilliant gold, his alpha wolf right under the skin, as he gave his brother a quick nod.

Nova kissed Landon again, her tongue dancing with his. Until they both claimed her, she would take the lead in the bedroom. She was running on instinct, doing her best to make this work.

"I want you to lie down next to Sawyer. It's okay if you want to take care of yourself."

Even though she'd told Landon it wasn't a punishment, she knew he would look it at that way before it was all over, but she was sure he would never tease Sawyer with his 'charming card' ever again.

Kneeling between Sawyer's legs, she cupped him with one hand and slowly stroked him with the other. He groaned in pleasure as his eyes fluttered close. Nova gripped the base of his cock and lowered her head to taste him. She took him into her mouth, and his body bucked under her ministrations. Sawyer was so responsive, and she delighted in taking his arousal to higher levels. He thrust into her mouth, and she rewarded him with licks and long pulls on the hard length of his erection. Using her hands and mouth on his shaft, Nova brought Sawyer to a frenzy of passion. His fingers knotted in her hair, working her head up and down, bringing him closer to release. She sucked him hard, and with a bone-deep growl of pleasure, he released deep in her throat.

Nova slid over his body to capture his mouth, possessing it, her tongue tasting his desire. At the same time, Landon pressed against her from behind, kissing her shoulders and neck while his hands roamed freely over her body, settling on the cheeks of her rounded ass. She *did* say he could touch and kiss, and Landon was proving to be as adept with his hands as his brother. Long, strong fingers found their way between her folds, and she sighed with pleasure into Sawyer's mouth, who held her tightly against his chest, never stopping the kiss as his arousal hardened against her belly.

Her body was on fire with pleasure, and she luxuriated in the sweet sensation. As Landon worked his magic with his fingers, she ground against Sawyer, mewling into his mouth as her need for release grew. Sawyer's hands weren't idle any longer, fondling her breasts and pinching her nipples with just the right amount of pain, making her cry out with need.

In a seamless move, Sawyer lifted her onto his erection, and Landon knelt between Sawyer's legs, his hands roaming over her body, settling between her folds again, working her clit as Sawyer thrust inside her in a steady rhythm. Nova was dizzy with desire as she gasped with pleasure over and over. With liquid fire singing in her veins, she gave in to the storm releasing through her. The orgasm was intense, and mindless ecstasy gripped her. Sawyer's climax shot through her, and a white-hot heat filled her. Landon never slowed, bringing her to yet another wild orgasm, ripping through her as she thrashed against him.

Collapsing against Landon's chest, he kissed her softly on the lips, then pushed her down gently into Sawyer's waiting arms. Sawyer captured her mouth with a kiss so full of passion and need, it almost brought her to tears.

How had she doubted that she could handle two mates? She had two skilled lovers who made sure she was pleasured in every way. It would only get better, and Nova couldn't imagine one male without the other. Obviously, the Goddess knew what she'd been doing all along.

Pounding on the door woke Nova from a sound sleep. Extricating herself from the puppy pile on the bed, she slipped on sweats and someone's t-shirt, Sawyer's by the scent of it, and made her way down the stairs.

Opening the door to a howling wind and a flurry of white, the two people bundled against the elements were almost unrecognizable, but Nova would've known her parents anywhere. Ushering them in, she shut the door hurriedly against the freezing cold.

"What in the world are you two doing out in this weather?" Nova asked in disbelief.

She wasted no time in setting up a carafe of coffee for her parents. Anything important enough to get her dad and mom out here would require a lot of caffeine.

Jace and Willow shed their outerwear and hung them on wall pegs by the front door. Following Nova into the kitchen, Jace slid onto a barstool while Willow hugged her daughter and studied her with a practiced motherly eye. Pushing Nova's hair back, her gaze rested on the mark.

"You're mated?"

Jace inhaled deeply, a low growl rumbling from deep within.

"I take it one of your houseguests is taking advantage of the situation?"

"Dad! It's not like that. Sawyer is my Fated Mate." Nova met her mother's gaze, silently begging for understanding. "I wanted to talk to you first, but there was so much to deal with, I never got the chance."

Willow kissed Nova on the cheek, then joined her mate at the kitchen bar.

"Why don't you fill us in now?" Willow glanced at the coffee pot. "We could all use a mug of something hot."

"I guess I should start with the elephant in the room then." Nova grabbed mugs for her parents and poured the coffee. "Sawyer is my Fated Mate," —she took a deep breath— "and so is Landon, his brother."

"Both of them?" Jace exploded.

A knowing smile crossed Willow's face as she sipped her coffee.

"It's not unheard of, Jace. You merely don't want to share your precious girls."

"You can't hold that against me, Willow, but Nova is special. I'm grooming her to be Alpha... how do I deal with two mates?"

"Dad, I'm no more special than Reagan or Lena. I just happen to be the oldest. If I ever become Alpha, having two mates won't matter. If anything, I'll have two loyal males at my side no one will be able to turn against me."

"She has a point, Jace."

"Very well. It's not like I can fight Fate." Nova's father sighed heavily. "You said they were both your mates, but I only scent the mark of one. What about the other one?"

"Sawyer has claimed me. Landon was the one who was injured."

"He's the main reason we're here. I wanted to know how his condition is," Jace added.

"Last night, the last of the silver was flushed from his system. This morning, he joined Sawyer and me in bed, in wolf form."

"I'm relieved to hear it, doubly so, now that I know he's one of your Fated Mates," Jace said sincerely. "According to Bryce and Linc, your male was in bad shape. We studied the trap... that was a nasty piece of business." He grimaced in distaste.

"Did you come up with anything about the trap?" Nova asked.

"Other than agreeing with you about it being infused with magic, not yet." He shook his head, then lifted a finger in the air. "I do know someone who I think can help. As soon as this storm lifts, I'm going to contact her and see if she would be willing to track down the source."

"So, you don't have any idea who could be setting silver traps on the mountain?"

"I've got a few ideas, even a hunch or two, but no proof," Jace admitted. "I'm not pointing fingers unless I'm one hundred percent sure. No sense in starting a war if it's not needed."

"You think it could escalate into war?" Nova didn't expect that response, and it shocked her.

"It depends on who's doing it and why."

Willow gathered the empty mugs and brought them to the sink. As she turned around, she smiled, and Nova looked to see what had captured her mother's attention. Sawyer and Landon were making their way down the stairs. Nova crossed the room and took their hands, leading them to her parents.

"Mom, Dad, I'd like you to meet my mates, Sawyer and Landon."

Jace stood, facing the two males. He rolled his shoulders, a surge of power filling the air.

Nova stilled, clutching her mates' hands tightly. Even though Sawyer and Landon were her Fated Mates, her father was Alpha, and it was his decision whether or not to accept the males into their pack. She held her breath, waiting to see what would happen in the next few moments.

Sawyer squeezed her hand and opened the bond between them, reassuring her everything would be fine. He stepped forward, with Landon following, a step behind. Both males approached the Alpha, eyes down and necks bared in submission.

"My daughter explained why you were on my mountain without permission, so I'll let that one slide," Jace growled. "The fact you are both her Fated Mates allows you some leeway, but not all. Identify yourselves to me, Jace Adkins, Alpha of the Bighorn Mountain pack."

Fear clutched at Nova's throat, making it hard for her to breathe. Her father was in full Alpha mode. She was sure Sawyer would gain her father's approval, but she wasn't as confident about Landon. She didn't know him well enough yet to make that call.

"My name is Sawyer Billings, formerly of the River Ridge pack. I no longer associate myself with the pack, claiming lone wolf status."

Jace studied Sawyer carefully as he spoke, weighing his words for truth. With a curt nod, he turned to Landon.

"My name is Landon Monroe, formerly of the River Ridge pack. I, too, claim lone wolf status, preferring to stay with my clan brother and friend."

"Clan brother? You are not blood brothers?"

"No, Alpha," Sawyer replied. "My parents took Landon in when he was a pup and raised him as their own. He's my best friend and brother in all ways except blood."

Jace stared at the two males hard, then glanced at Nova, his gaze searching her face, his pack bond opening to her, searching her heart as well. With a soft exhale, he turned back to his daughter's mates.

"You are my daughter's Fated Mates, and I welcome you as family. I accept you as pack and will introduce you to everyone on the next full moon." Jace dropped the power roll he'd been holding over the room and extended a hand to each man. "Cherish my daughter. She's precious to me and her mother."

10

Nova didn't wait to watch her parents leave as she usually did. The air was bitterly cold, biting bone deep. She barely heard the roar of the snowmobiles over the howling wind and prayed her parents traveled safely. She'd made her mom promise to call as soon as they were home.

"You seem a little preoccupied," Sawyer observed. "Did your visit not go well with your parents before we came downstairs?"

"What? Oh, no, the visit was fine. I was thinking about something Dad said earlier."

Sawyer wrapped her in his arms and kissed her softly on the lips.

"Something about us?"

She smiled up at him and caressed his cheek.

"No, if he has something to say about you, he'll tell you to your face. You never have to worry about him trash talking behind your back."

"Good to know," Sawyer said lightly, capturing her hand and leading her back to the kitchen. "Landon is fixing us a late breakfast. Come sit down while we get everything together, and you can tell us what's worrying you."

Landon looked up as they approached, a shy smile on his face. He picked up a grape from the fruit he was sorting and brought it to Nova. He kissed her, then offered her the grape.

"How do you like your bacon?"

"Crispy, please." The sweetness of the fruit splashed on her tongue and a tiny moan of pleasure escaped her lips. "Grapes aren't even in season. How did we manage to get some so sweet?" Nova exclaimed.

"Lucky, I guess," Landon shrugged. "They were in the fridge along with some other fruit."

"The fruit came from Linc and Bryce. It was in the box of groceries they left on the counter," Sawyer told her as he popped a strawberry in his mouth.

"They must have come from Linc's mate, Della. She grows a lot of fruit and vegetables hydroponically. In fact, she's gotten so good at it, there's usually enough for everyone."

"That's a valuable asset to any pack," Landon noted.

"It is," Nova agreed. "Especially up here in the mountains. We don't exactly have fertile farmland around here."

Sawyer arched a brow, reminding her he was still waiting for her to tell them what her father had said.

"I asked my father about the bear trap and if he'd figured anything out yet. He said he knew someone who could probably help him, and he would contact her tomorrow if the weather let up."

"Help him in what way?" Sawyer asked.

"Dad agrees with me that the steel was magically infused with silver. In that case, the best person to be able to help would be a witch. He's on speaking terms with a couple of covens, so I'm guessing he's going to reach out to one or both of them."

"Would they actually help him?" Landon poured the batter into the skillet, making perfectly round pancakes. "I mean, if it's magic we're dealing with, wouldn't the witches be turning on one of their own?"

"It's a slippery slope,"—Nova nodded in agreement—"but Dad has had a long running relationship with the covens, and they owe him favors. So, if anyone can get them to talk, it will be him."

"Sounds like your dad is a powerful male."

"He's Alpha of Bighorn Mountain for a reason," Nova said thoughtfully. "Not many are foolish enough to cross him. He has the numbers to back him if push comes to shove."

"That's definitely in his favor," Sawyer said. "Though, the more powerful one is, the more enemies they tend to make. It's the way the world works."

"You're not wrong, and Dad did say he had an idea or two who was behind it, but he wasn't prepared to say anything without proof."

"That's what actually has you worried, isn't it?" Landon asked.

Nova looked up in surprise. Landon was a lot more astute than what she'd given him credit for. She wouldn't underestimate her mate again.

"More than I'd like to admit," Nova nodded as she fixed another mug of coffee. "He's worried the situation could start a war, depending on who planted the traps. It's not good for any of us. There are a handful of shifter clans and packs on the mountain and a few other supernaturals as well. We've managed to live peacefully together until now. I'd hate to see that fall apart."

"That kind of fallout could spill over into the human population," Sawyer noted. "We'd have a mess there'd be no coming back from."

"So, not only do we have to find out who's responsible, but we also have to contain the situation as soon as possible." Landon served plates stacked high with pancakes and bacon to Sawyer and Nova. "How can Sawyer and I help your dad?"

"You found the trap, as painful as that was. We didn't even know there was a problem before then." Nova smiled widely, her fork poised in the air. Sawyer's concern and worry flowed through their bond, and she sensed Landon felt the same. "For now, all we can do is wait. When Dad gets a plan together, he'll let us know what we can do. I appreciate the two of you jumping in like this. It means a lot."

"We're your mates," Sawyer said softly. "I know we haven't discussed logistics yet, but I'm reasonably sure this is going to be our home, and we'll protect it… and you, with our lives."

"What he said." Landon winked as he popped a strawberry into his mouth.

Jace clamped down on the urge to pace while the witch carefully inspected the bear trap. She'd been staring at it, turning it around and around in her hands, for at least ten minutes without saying a word. He was a patient man, but she was testing him… not that he would ever let her know that.

Miriam Bishop, High Priestess of the Dark Forest coven, carefully set the steel trap down on the table beside her and looked up. Long, black hair framed a stern but attractive face, and a knowing smile showed a vast knowledge, most of it secretive.

"You were right in your assumption of magic being used. It's heavily infused with silver, which could only be done by someone with powerful magic."

"Is there anyway you can trace it to the source or who planted it in the woods? I need to ferret out the culprit before anyone else is hurt. It's bad enough one of my daughter's Fated Mates almost died from silver poisoning."

"It would have been catastrophic for Nova and her remaining mate. We can thank the Goddess she had other plans for your daughter." Miriam rose, crossing the room to stare out the window. "As for the source, I can't tell. I do know it was handled by a bear shifter, his imprint is quite strong. Perhaps if you narrow down the shifter, I could tell you which magic wielder they hired for this kind of work."

"A bear shifter?" Jace stilled, pieces of the puzzle falling into place. "If that's the case, I may be able to have the information for you shortly." He rose and crossed the room to face the witch, an envelope in his hand. "Once again, your help has been invaluable," handing her the agreed-upon payment.

"Is there anything else I can help you with?"

"Not at the moment, but I'll contact you if the need arises."

"Glad to be of help, Alpha. I hope you can clear up this situation swiftly."

The witch vanished in a swirl of motion and color. Damn handy bit of magic to have, especially in this kind of weather. Jace scented the air and traced the familiar fragrance to the living room, where his mate waited. As Alpha, he kept too many secrets and far too much information close to the vest, but there were times when he needed to share with his mate— this was one of those times.

"Was Miriam able to help you?" Willow looked up from the book she'd been reading, smiled at him warmly, and set the book on a nearby table as she patted the sofa cushion beside her.

Jace draped an arm around his mate as he sat. Her fragrance surrounded him, calming him as it always did. Willow was so much more than his Fated Mate. She was his north star, the ground beneath his feet, and the wings with which he soared. He hoped Nova would know this kind of love with her own mates, for it made each day an adventure to be shared.

"She did, in a roundabout way," Jace replied. "She was able to tell me a bear shifter handled the trap, and if I could pin down which one, she could find the magic wielder who infused the metal with silver."

"A bear shifter?" Willow paled, a hand going to her throat. "You're thinking Baron had something to do with this?"

"I have to admit it was my first thought, but I need to do more digging before I say anything."

"I don't understand, Jace. He wanted Nova as his mate. Why in the world would he do something to hurt the pack?"

The confusion and fear coming from his mate tore at him, and his wolf lunged to the surface to protect.

"Let's not jump to conclusions. As I said, I need more information, but if I find out he set the trap to hurt one of us as revenge for me turning him down, he's going to wish he'd never climbed this mountain. I'll take him down and his whole sleuth with him."

11

Landon stomped the snow from his boots on the porch before he went inside with the firewood. The storm had passed, leaving a bitterly cold world of snow and ice. Looking up, he wondered when the sun would make an appearance because these gray and dreary days were wearing on him and his wolf.

Adding logs to the fire, he stoked the flames higher, cursing under his breath when he shoved a log too hard, and sparks flew out. Hurrying to put the screen back in place, Landon stretched and glanced up the stairs where Nova and Sawyer were still sleeping.

It had been days since he'd shifted, and thankfully free of the silver that had poisoned his system. He was back to his normal self and restless as any penned-up animal. He needed to be outdoors where his wolf could run off some steam. The frustration of having a Fated Mate and not being able to claim her was driving his wolf crazy… which was making him on edge.

He honestly didn't know if he could handle another night of watching Sawyer make love to Nova, and not be a true part of the union. He understood what Nova was doing, but it didn't make it any easier to deal with. He wanted more than touches and kisses… he wanted to be inside her, to share her fully with his brother, to claim her as his mate. Damn it all to hell and back, he *needed* his mates.

Tearing off his clothes, he threw them in a pile next to the front door. He bit off a curse as the wind tore at his naked flesh, shriveling the hard-on he'd gotten thinking about Nova and Sawyer. *Guess that was one way of dealing with it.* Shifting to his wolf, Landon leapt off the porch and bounded off through the snow. He needed to run, but he needed to be careful, not wanting to land in another trap. He wasn't foolish enough to think there was only one planted out there.

Keeping to wide open areas, Landon ran, sometimes sinking in soft patches of snow, but able to shake free and continue his trek across the snowy expanse of land. The cold air bit his lungs when he drew in deep breaths, but it was exhilarating to be out and free to run. For now, the clamor in his head to claim his mate had abated, and a sense of peace filled him… something he'd been missing for longer than he'd realized.

He gave his wolf free rein to be himself, sniffing at trees, jumping logs, and rolling in the snow like a pup. Shaking the snow free from his coat, Landon circled back, headed to the cabin. With his mind clearer than it had been in weeks, the demands imposed on him by his Fated Mates would no longer be such a hardship.

A strange scent caught his attention and Landon tensed, in full alert. Skirting across the open field, he raced to the side of the garage, planning on checking the perimeter of the house before he went inside. A huge pawprint in the snow on the side of the house brought him up short. One sniff and he knew it was a bear, though it made no sense. Bears hibernated in the winter, there was no reason for one to be wandering around, especially this close to a building—unless it was a shifter.

He needed to alert Sawyer and talk to Nova. If there was a bear shifter skulking about, his mates needed to know about it, and they needed to deal with the situation. Landon wouldn't allow his mates to be in harm's way.

Nova whirled around when the front door opened and a naked Landon came barreling through, slamming the door shut behind him.

"Where have you been?" she cried out, fear and worry making her heart race.

"Out for a run… I'll explain later." Landon hurriedly dressed as he glanced around the room. "Where's Sawyer? I need you two to come outside and see this. We may have trouble."

"I'm right here," Sawyer said, coming from the kitchen. One look at Landon and he set his coffee down and grabbed his boots.

Nova could sense Landon's urgency, but she could feel Sawyer's anxiety rise, so she followed suit, bundling up as fast as she could. Within minutes, the trio was outside, tramping toward the side of the house.

Paw prints deeply embedded in the snow were right outside the kitchen, a row of tracks leading away from the house toward the forest. Nova stared off into the distance, looking for any sign of what could have made the prints but found no movement of any kind.

"Should we follow the tracks?" Landon asked, as he crouched down before the largest print. His fingers sunk into a crevice a good three inches deep. "This is a huge beast. I thought there were only black bears in this area."

"There are black bears of the animal variety around here, but there are a couple of bear shifters on the mountain." Nova hugged herself against the biting cold. "There's a clan of black bears on the other side of the mountain that have been here forever, and there's a sleuth of grizzlies farther up the mountain, but they tend to keep to themselves."

"Any idea why one of them would come snooping around your place?" Sawyer asked.

"Not a clue." Nova stomped her feet to circulate some warmth. "Look, I don't want you guys going after whatever made those tracks. Let me call Dad and tell him what we found."

Sawyer's expression shuttered close, and Nova inwardly cursed. Sawyer was beginning to rediscover his alpha persona, and she'd shut him down with a mention of her father. Closing the distance between them, Nova captured his hands.

"I'm not doubting you and Landon can handle this, but there's more at stake. There's something going on, and the Alpha has to be notified. Besides, I don't think I could deal with something happening to either of you."

Sawyer wrapped his arms around her and kissed the tip of her nose. The warmth of his lips felt good on her cold skin.

"You're right. We'll call your father first. It's best if we play it safe for now." Sawyer gestured to Landon. "Take a picture of the print and let's get back inside. No sense in freezing out here any longer."

Nova was on the phone with her dad when Landon walked in and handed her his phone with several images of the print on the screen.

"I'm texting you the photos Landon took of the tracks outside the house," Nova informed her father.

"I don't know what's going on, but I don't need any bears skulking around my house... shifters or not."

She caught the exchange of furtive looks between her mates and nervously chewed on her bottom lip. The last thing she wanted was for them to try to track down the prints. They weren't familiar with the mountain terrain and the thought of more silver-laced traps did nothing to allay her fears.

Nova ended the call and slipped her cell phone into the back pocket of her jeans. Before she could get her thoughts together, Sawyer was in front of her, a curled finger tipping her head up to meet his gaze.

"What's going on?"

"I honestly don't know." She wasn't lying. Her father had left so much unsaid, and it bothered her more than she liked. "There's something he's not telling me, and that's not like him."

"Do you know any of those bear shifters?" Landon asked.

"Not really. I've met Baron Cooper, the leader of the sleuth of grizzlies, but I've never had any personal dealings with the man. He's too arrogant for my taste, even as an alpha."

"What precisely *did* your father say?"

Nova inwardly squirmed under Sawyer's unrelenting stare. She had to choose her words carefully with him when it came to orders from her father. He would follow the Alpha's directives, that wasn't the problem. It was how she treated him as a mate and an alpha in his own right. She was trying to repair years of damage to his wolf's alpha identity, and it wasn't going to happen in a few days.

"He wants us to stick close to the cabin, and if we do go outside, have someone with us. He doesn't want us to take any chances of being blindsided."

"There's definitely more going on than what he's telling you," Landon said.

"Yeah, and that means no more disappearing acts from you." Sawyer rounded on his brother. "You scared the crap out of Nova and had us both worried."

"I know... I'm sorry, but I had to get out for a while." Landon ran a hand through his short locks. "Everything was getting to me..." he faltered.

"This is my fault, isn't it?" Nova asked softly, crossing the room to face Landon.

"It's not a matter of fault... I don't blame you for anything." Landon struggled to explain his feelings. "Waiting for you to accept me is harder than I realized it would be, and my wolf wasn't making it any easier."

Nova glanced at Sawyer, who gave her a short nod. She sighed, more in relief than anything else. She'd gone too far, had hurt one mate because she'd sided with the other, though she swore it was something she'd never do. Nova had to make things right, and that meant letting Landon claim her.

She was falling in love with him, it wasn't even a question. The past few days had shown her a kind and loving male, one whose loyalty would never be misplaced or doubted.

He wasn't as settled as Sawyer was, but there was a ten-year difference between them, and that accounted for a lot. Landon and Sawyer were two very different males, but they had one thing in common—they were her Fated Mates, and she owed them all her love and devotion.

"I'm so sorry, Landon. I need to make things right, and the first thing is to let you claim me. How about we take care of that now?" She smiled up at him, searching his face for forgiveness.

Landon glanced over at Sawyer who shook his head.

"Go on. It's only fair this be between the two of you. Claim your mate, brother. We have a lifetime to share."

"Come, it's our turn." Nova kissed him tenderly, her tongue delving between his lips.

Draping an arm around Nova's shoulders, Landon led her up the stairs.

Closing the bedroom door behind them, Nova found Landon watching her closely. She'd been taking the lead in bed, and now found herself wanting to let Landon take over. He may not be alpha, but he was definitely as important to her as Sawyer, and she wanted this first time to be special for them both.

"Tell me what you want."

Landon swallowed hard, realization of the gift she'd given him dawning on his face. He framed her face with his hands, gazing deep into her eyes before softly kissing her forehead.

"I want to taste you. I want to be deep inside you. I want to make you mine." He slanted his mouth over hers, claiming her lips with a toe-curling kiss. "Then I want to do it all over again," he breathed into her mouth.

Nova moaned, her breaths already ragged from only a kiss.

"I want that, too. Make me yours, Landon."

"Take off your clothes, lie on the bed, and part your legs."

Nova arched a brow, but instead of a snarky retort, she licked her lips in a decidedly wicked way and did as ordered. She would give him this. Deep down, Nova also knew she would enjoy the role change. She was only beginning to discover the sexual pleasures her Fated Mates would bring to the bedroom… or anywhere else the mood took them.

She wasn't wearing sexy lingerie, but she'd damn well make him think it was a Victoria's Secret floor show before she finished, making each move as erotic and suggestive as possible. By the time she slithered onto the bed and lay spread-eagled, touching herself, he was hovering over her, stroking a very impressive erection.

"I've never seen a more beautiful sight in my entire life." Landon husked. His eyes flashed color, his wolf close at hand. "You take my breath away."

"Come here and let me breathe life into you," she purred seductively.

Lying beside her, Landon ravaged her mouth with kisses, his sharp need arousing her to a fever pitch. When she would have pulled him into her arms, he slid down the bed to kneel before her parted legs. He nuzzled the inside of her thigh, and Nova shivered with anticipation. Landon explored her with his tongue, lashing inside her, driving her wild with desire. She wanted more, she needed more.

His mouth never stopped working her wet center as she arched into him, crying for release, begging for him to fill her, to fuck her mindless. Nova thrashed under his masterful tongue and fingers until a white-hot climax ripped through her, leaving her gasping and shattered on the sheets.

Landon plunged into her wet heat, pulled out almost all the way, then thrust deep and hard, setting a rhythm she met thrust for thrust. Nova's nails raked his back as he stretched her with his manhood, crying out his name in pleasure. Hard, rough strokes rocked her body, and still she needed more.

Pulling out, he turned her over to her knees, entering from behind, a hand on the nape of her neck as he worked his girth inside her with an animal fierceness. Pleasure racked her body as he hammered into her, and she was trapped between torment and ecstasy. Every nerve in her body was on fire, alive with passion, need, and hunger for more.

When the climax came, it came for them both, hard and fast, heat and pleasure. With a shout, he thrust deep as razor-sharp canines bit into the junction of the opposite shoulder where Sawyer had claimed her. Stars burst behind her eyelids as the orgasm ripped through her.

Then, like magic, the mate bond opened, and Nova knew Landon in every way possible... his doubts, fears... how much he cared for Sawyer, and his love for her, which brought her to tears.

"You're crying. Did I hurt you?" Landon pulled her into his arms, holding her tight.

"Oh, no. It was perfect... *you* were perfect.

12

Nova braided her long hair and gave herself a once over in the full-length mirror. It was back to the real world, and she wasn't ready to leave her mates behind, even for the day, but she had a clinic to run, though she didn't expect a lot of business waiting for her.

The storm had abated, but winter was in full force, which kept the general population in their homes, safe and warm from nature's elements.

"Morning, beautiful. Do you have time for breakfast before you take off?" Landon asked from the bathroom doorway.

"Good morning yourself." She crossed the few steps to him for a leisurely kiss. "I'll pass on breakfast, but thanks. I've got granola bars stashed at the clinic. Nova chuckled when he frowned in disapproval. This mate liked to cook and enjoyed watching her eat.

"I've survived for years on granola bars. I'll be fine." Wrapping her arms around his waist, she pulled him close for another scorching kiss. "How about I make it up to you when I come home?"

"Are we talking dinner... or something else?" He smirked.

"Oh, I'm reasonably sure we can manage both." Her laugh was low and melodic. "But right now, I need to get going."

"Where's Sawyer?"

The bed was empty, rumpled sheets a testimony to their night's lovemaking.

"He's warming up the Jeep for you." Landon hurried on before she could protest. "I went with him to make sure the coast was clear."

"Promise me neither of you will take any chances, and you'll stay close to the cabin." She wasn't going to demand they stay inside, though the thought crossed her mind.

"When we come back, you have a deal."

"What do you mean?"

"We need to hitch a ride to our truck. All our gear and clothes are in it, and Sawyer needs to check on his clients."

"I'd forgotten all about that," Nova said. "Let me grab the spare key to the cabin while you get dressed."

On her way to the kitchen for her thermos and tote, Nova opened a drawer to the sideboard, picking up a ring of keys. Finding the extra house key, she slipped it off and gave it to Landon when he joined her. Boots, coat, gloves, and knit cap in place, she locked the door behind them and made her way to the garage to find Sawyer smiling at her from inside a vehicle already warmed up and ready to go.

Vacating the driver's seat, Sawyer went around to the passenger side while Landon slipped in the back. Easing out of the garage, Nova headed down the mountain, toward town. It didn't take long to get to Sawyer's truck, but it would take a few minutes to clear the snow around it. Nova refused to leave until she knew the truck was running and that they wouldn't be stranded.

With her mates following closely behind, Nova headed to her clinic. The guys were going to pick up a few things at the store, then head back to the cabin. Both had work to catch up on and promised her she had nothing to worry about. On that note, she breathed a little easier.

Business was light to nonexistent, as she'd guessed, so Nova spent the morning returning calls and scheduling visits for the coming weeks. At least it hadn't been a total waste of a day coming in. Around two o'clock the phone rang, and Nova closed the refrigerator, where she'd been doing an inventory of meds.

She'd barely answered when a rushed voice came over the line.

"Nova, this is Susan Coburn. I need your help. Shadow's in labor and she's in trouble."

"I'm on my way."

Nova didn't bother with questions she didn't need where Susan was concerned. Coburn Ranch had been her client since she started her practice, breeding and raising a quality line of cutting horses. Every mare on the property was worth a small fortune, and each foal was a potential champion. Shadow was one of Susan's personal favorites and the mare meant the world to the owner, as well as being one of the ranch's biggest sources of income. Her last foal had sold for a half-million dollars.

Locking the clinic up, Nova jumped into her Jeep. Thanks to her light morning, anything she would need was already in the vehicle. It would take a half-hour at least to get to Coburn Ranch and she didn't have time to waste.

Pulling into the ranch's gated entrance, she headed for the back barn which housed the broodmares. There was no activity around the barns, which was odd, but Nova put it down to the weather and thought nothing more of the matter.

Parking near the barn doors, she made her way to the opening. Usually, the doors were wide open but today they were only opened wide enough for a single person to walk through. Again, not the norm, but these high-dollar mares didn't need to be exposed to the winter winds either.

The familiar smell of fresh hay and sawdust surrounded her, and any uneasiness left as she looked around. Horses nickered at the sight of her, others munching contentedly on their hay. Walking down the long shed row, Nova headed for Shadow's stall.

As she approached the familiar surroundings, Susan stumbled out of a stall, a tall man holding her against him.

Strong arms caught Nova unawares and metal clamped around her wrists, leaving her unable to defend herself.

"I'm sorry, Nova. They made me call you," Susan cried out. "I swear I had nothing to do with it."

The burly man pushed Susan, who fell hard against the opposite stall. She lay in a heap on the ground, motionless.

"She served her purpose, leave her there," barked the man, when one of the others went to aid the woman.

"Who are you, and what's the meaning of this?" Nova struggled against her bindings.

"You'll know everything soon enough." The man dished out orders like a general. "Get her in the truck. We got what we came for."

Nova was gagged and a hood placed over her head as she was guided out the barn and into a vehicle. Fighting was useless, so Nova struggled to remain calm and use her other senses to figure out where they were taking her. Once the truck started moving, she knew one thing for sure... she was the only wolf in a vehicle filled with bears.

"You're going to make a rut in the floor if you don't stop pacing," Landon observed from the kitchen.

"I can't help it. Nova should've been back by now... or at least called."

"She might have got tied up with an emergency. She doesn't exactly have office hours."

"You're right, or at least that's what I keep telling myself, but I can't stop feeling like something's wrong." He stopped and stared at his brother. "You don't feel it?"

Landon placed the lid on the pot and turned to face him.

"Yeah, I feel it, but you've got enough anxiety going for both of us."

"I don't know what to do, and I hate feeling this helpless," Sawyer snapped. "I've called a half-dozen times, and they all go straight to voice mail."

Landon glanced at the clock on the kitchen wall. It was nearing six in the evening and was already dark outside.

"We could drive down to the clinic and see if she's there," Landon suggested.

"Yeah, I suppose, though part of me hates to leave."

"There's only one way up here, we'd see her if she was headed this way."

"True, and I remember the alarm sequence and keypad code so we can get in if she's not there. She might have left an address lying around."

"It's better than sitting here and watching you pace. Let's go." Landon turned off the stove and headed for the coat rack.

Within minutes, they headed down the road toward town. Luckily, it hadn't snowed yet, but that didn't mean it wouldn't. Sawyer gripped the steering wheel and focused on the narrow road. The last thing he needed was to run off the path and either hit something or get stuck—either scenario would be a disaster.

"Should we call Nova's dad?" Landon's voice was low, but Sawyer sensed the worry creeping through.

"Let's wait till we get to the clinic. I don't want to alarm the Alpha unnecessarily." He glanced at his brother. "This is not quite how I wanted our relationship to start off."

"You have a point." Landon met his gaze. "Who wants to tell the Alpha we lost his daughter the first day she went back to work?"

"Technically, we didn't lose her."

"It's not gonna make a damn bit of difference to Nova's father."

"You got that right," Sawyer groaned.

The rest of the ride was made in silence, each lost in their thoughts but both thinking of their mate.

Sawyer pulled into the small parking lot on the side of the clinic and slammed both hands against the steering wheel.

"She's not here, and going by the snow on the lot, no one has been here in a while."

"Let's go inside and see if we can find out anything," Landon suggested.

"I hope there's some kind of clue in there." Sawyer yanked on his cap as he exited the truck. "Because if there's not, I have no idea how to find her."

Sawyer opened the back door to the clinic to find the lights off. Feeling around, he located a switch and flipped it, bathing the room in soft light. Landon walked past him and looked around.

"Looks like she locked up and left."

"Yeah, and that's not good for us. Let's find her office. She might have left something on her desk that could help us track her down."

The clinic wasn't large, but they still had to open a few doors before they found Nova's office. As organized and spotless as the rest of the rooms, Sawyer's heart sank when it appeared there wouldn't be anything to tell them where she'd gone.

Landon was studying her desk calendar when he looked up sharply and motioned to Sawyer.

"I think I found something." He pointed at the day's date, and Coburn Ranch was circled in red. "If we can find a number for this Coburn Ranch, we can call and see if she's there."

Sawyer opened a filing cabinet and rifled through the files, pulling out a thick red folder.

"Here we go. Coburn Ranch, cutting horse breeder. There's a number and an address." Setting the folder down on the desk, he punched the number into his phone and waited for the call to connect. After six rings, it patched through to voice mail.

"Put this address in your phone's GPS. It looks like we're going to Coburn Ranch. No one answered the phone."

Thanks to the GPS, it wasn't difficult to get to the ranch, but pitch-dark skies and unfamiliar roads slowed Sawyer's driving down to a crawl. Passing through the gates of the ranch lay a sprawling configuration of houses and barns.

"Where do we even start?" Landon groaned. "As big as this place is, there should be lights on, at least at the main house."

"You would think," Sawyer agreed. "Wait, look up there. Isn't that Nova's truck parked by that barn?"

"Yeah, it is. At last, we're getting somewhere." Landon leaned forward, hands braced against the dash.

Parking beside the Jeep, Sawyer and Landon wasted no time entering the barn. Horses neighed and whinnied at their approach, some kicking stall walls.

"Looks like someone missed their feeding time."

Sawyer inhaled deeply, fresh hay and sawdust permeating the air, but there was something else too... faint, but familiar.

"Down here." Sawyer ran down the shed row, searching for Nova's scent. As they approached the end of the stalls, Landon veered off to the right. A crumpled form lay on the ground.

"Is it Nova?" Sawyer asked, holding his breath.

"No, it's a woman, and she's alive."

Rushing to Landon's side, Sawyer helped his brother gently turn the woman over. Caked blood covered the side of her face, a nasty gash at her hairline.

"Ma'am? Can you hear me?" Sawyer tapped her cheeks as he spoke, trying to rouse her. He breathed a sigh of relief when her eyelids fluttered.

"Who... who are you? What happened?" the woman gasped.

"My name is Sawyer Billings, and this is Landon Monroe. We've come looking for Nova Adkins. Do you know where she is?"

"Nova?" The woman's eyes widened in fear as she struggled to sit up. "Nova! Oh, my god. They took her!"

"Who took her?" Sawyer asked, his worst fears rising to the surface.

"I... I don't know who they were. They cornered me in the barn and made me fake an emergency to get her out here. The man pushed me, and I fell... I don't know what happened after that."

"Landon, call Jace and have him meet us out here. We've got a problem."

13

Sawyer tended to the woman's head wound and helped her to the barn phone, so she could call her daughter and son-in-law to tend to the horses. They sat together talking quietly as Landon approached.

"Jace is on the way. He said not to call the cops. He'll deal with it himself." Landon made eye contact with the woman. "Jace Adkins is Nova's father, and we have a feeling he knows who's responsible for this."

"I don't understand." Susan gingerly touched the bandage on her head. "Who would want to hurt Nova? Everyone loves her."

"We don't know either, but I can promise we're going to find Nova and the ones responsible for this."

Sawyer tried to keep the woman calm until her family showed up to care for her.

"They *will* pay," Landon assured her.

A young couple jogged down the shed row toward them, speeding up when they saw Susan stand with the aid of Sawyer. After filling them in the best they could, the daughter helped Susan home while her husband tended to a barn full of impatient and hungry horses.

Sawyer and Landon stood in the open doorway of the barn when the headlights of several vehicles cut through the dark night.

"Looks like he brought reinforcements." Landon squinted against the glare of headlights.

"I didn't expect less. Nova is his oldest and being groomed to become Alpha, he's not going to take this lightly."

Jace Adkins strode into the barn followed by a half-dozen muscular males, all towering over six feet with ferocious scowls on their faces. Other than the Alpha, Bryce and Linc were the only other familiar faces that Sawyer recognized.

"Spread out and look for anything that can be traced to these assholes. Find Nova's scent so we can figure out who took her and where they went."

Jace cut a lethal glare toward Sawyer and Landon, then exhaled a deep breath as he approached them, shaking their hands.

"Were you able to find out anything from the woman who owns this place?"

"Not enough for us to go on," Sawyer faced the Alpha with a level look, though it took everything he had to do it. Nova was *their* mate, and he wasn't going to let anyone shove him and Landon aside in the search to find her.

"Susan said three men showed up and threatened to start shooting horses if she didn't call Nova here on pretense of an emergency call. Since Nova is her regular vet, a phone call was all it took. She also said the men were careful not to use names, but one of them slipped and called the leader, Fritz. She acted like she hadn't heard but remembered it because it wasn't a regular name, especially around here."

"Fritz, huh?"

"There's only one male by that name around these parts." The speaker stepped out of the shadows and approached them. The male was massive, with long, brown hair flowing out from under his knit cap.

"Sawyer, Landon, this is my Beta, Troy Jenkins." The males shook hands at the introduction. "Troy is one of the best trackers around these parts."

"That stall over there,"—Troy pointed to the end stall—"stinks of bear, and if it's the same Fritz, then we have a winner."

"Baron Cooper." Jace spat on the ground. "I should have known. Couldn't take no for an answer."

"What do you mean... couldn't take no for an answer?" Landon asked.

"Nova's mentioned this Cooper character before. She doesn't care for him," Sawyer added.

"Cooper came by my place a while back. His sleuth was having scuffles with the black bear clan, and he wanted to forge an alliance with me in case trouble escalated, but he wanted to mate with my eldest daughter to ensure I didn't back out of the deal."

"Bet that went over well with Nova," Sawyer bit out.

"I never told her," Jace said with a sigh. "I turned Cooper down flat. I've got no grief with the black bears. They've been on this mountain as long as, if not longer, than us. They're peaceful shifters and keep to themselves."

"I never saw this coming." Jace scrubbed his face. "He's got nothing to gain by it."

"Then I guess the question is, does he want Nova for a mate, or does he want revenge?"

"Going by the fact she's already wearing two mate marks, I think we need to get to her pronto," Troy warned.

"There's no doubt about it, but we have to be smart how we deal with the situation. If we go crashing up the mountain into his territory, they'll kill Nova before we even get close." Jace snarled his frustration. "Let's head back home and regroup," he ordered. "We're going to need the pack for this one."

Unable to speak, see, or move around, Nova seethed in silence. The males in the vehicle kept conversation to a minimum, giving her nothing to go on. By the movement of the truck, she knew they were climbing the mountain, but it still left a lot of territory to cover.

She worried about Susan and if she was all right. The woman had fallen hard, hitting her head against a stall wall. While there were ranch hands living on the property, Susan preferred to tend to the horses herself, so no one would venture into the barn until morning.

By this time, Sawyer and Landon would be worried she hadn't come home. She berated herself for not letting them know she'd gone out on a call. They would have no idea where she was. Not that the information would've done them any good, seeing she'd been abducted and was on the way to who knew where.

The truck lurched to a standstill, and the engine cut off. Nova guessed they'd reached their destination when the males exited, and she heard muffled conversation nearby. Strong hands reached in, pulling her from the truck. The hood was snatched from her head, and she strained to see where she was.

She took in a couple of log homes set back in a clearing around an enormous firepit before one of the males pushed her forward. Stumbling over the rough ground, Nova fought to keep her balance as her guards led her toward the house on the left. Entering the dwelling, she was led to a chair in the middle of the room.

"Sit. He'll be with you shortly."

She would have asked who *he* was, but the gag was still in place and her hands were cuffed behind her back.

"I see my esteemed guest has finally arrived."

The voice was vaguely familiar. Nova cautiously turned in her chair to see who had spoken. The figure was hidden in the shadows, and she couldn't make out who it was. Jutting her chin out and staring defiantly at the shrouded figure, she waited.

"Your father said you had a mind of your own." The speaker laughed low. "I wouldn't mind taming that little wild streak."

He stepped out into the open and Nova recognized him immediately, her eyes widening in surprise. Crossing over to her, he pulled the gag out of her mouth, his eyes pinning her with amusement and something she'd rather not put a name to.

"Baron Cooper! *You're* responsible for this?" Nova spat. "My father is going to have your hide on his den floor when he catches up to you!"

"Ouch! That's a bit harsh, don't you think?" The bear shifter smirked. "This could have all been settled reasonably when I spoke with your father about you becoming my mate..." Baron sniffed the air, then inhaled deeply, a frown creasing his rugged features. Standing in front of Nova, he opened her coat and tore at the opening of her shirt, exposing the two mate marks.

"You're mated already?" He roared. "To *two* males?" He slapped her across the face so hard she fell over backward, rolling onto the floor. "I'll make you watch the life fade from their eyes when I kill them both. You were supposed to be *my* mate!"

Without the use of her arms, Nova had no way to brace herself for the fall, hitting the floor with a thud. She tried to roll away from Baron, but he was too fast for her, pulling her up by a bound arm. Righting the chair, he pushed Nova back onto it.

"You thought you pulled a fast one on me… getting mated before our mating was announced."

"What are you talking about?" Nova snapped. "I was never going to mate with you. I don't even know you."

Baron stilled, staring at her from under hooded lids. Then he laughed, a sound that grated on Nova's ears.

"He didn't tell you!" Baron whirled around to meet her stare. "Your father never said a word about me, did he?"

Nova had no idea what this lunatic was talking about. Her father didn't believe in arranged marriages or power matings. They'd talked about it before, and he swore he would never make her or her sisters mate with someone they hadn't chosen for themselves. There was no way he would've changed his mind and not said something to her first.

"I requested an alliance with your father, ensuring my place on Bighorn. When I suggested mating with you to further seal the deal, he turned me down," Baron explained matter-of-factly.

The shifter paced in front of her, becoming more agitated as his story progressed.

“I’m not one to accept rejection. If we were mated, he would have to accept me as an ally. After all, he’s not going to turn against his own, is he?” Baron leered at her, making Nova’s skin crawl. “I go to all the trouble to have you brought to me and what do I find? You’ve already mated to another… to two males! One isn’t enough for you? I never figured you for a whore.”

Nova bit back a scalding retort. He was already irate, lost in the madness of his own mind. She wasn’t going to escalate the situation.

“But I can get around this, too. All I have to do is eliminate the problem. If your mates are dead, the marks will fade… then I can claim you for my own. I’m sure your mates are searching for you by now. If you’ll excuse me, I need to see to my dilemma.”

Nova blinked back tears. The male was mad as a hatter. She had to find a way to get out of here before he figured out who her mates were. Sawyer and Landon had no way of knowing their lives were in danger.

14

Sawyer fell into line behind Jace's truck for the ride back. He was worried, scared, and unsure of what was to come. He was so lost in his thoughts he didn't hear Landon talking at first.

"Sawyer!" Landon slapped his brother's arm, trying to get his attention.

"What? I'm sorry… you said something?"

"I asked if you could feel Nova through your mate bond? I know she's alive but not much else."

Sawyer tried to focus on the link he had with his Fated Mate. Like Landon, he knew she was alive, but he couldn't feel her emotions.

"No more than what you can. It's likely distance plays into it." He shrugged. "I don't actually know how this mate bond works. Nova was going to ask her mother about it, but I don't think she ever got the chance."

"If Jace never told her about Cooper's offer, she'll have no idea what's going on."

"Yeah, she's probably more pissed than scared right now."

"You're right about that." Landon chuckled bitterly.

"I've never known any woman more capable of taking care of herself than Nova." Sawyer wasn't sure if he wasn't trying to convince his brother or himself at this point.

"That's true, but she's with bear shifters. Those bastards are mean and vicious."

"Let's not dwell on the what ifs. Jace is going to come up with a plan, and we're going to get her out of there."

"I hope you're right because I'm lost right now, Sawyer. It's killing me to admit it, but I don't know what to do in this kind of situation. I'm not prepared."

"That's my fault, and I'm sorry. You should have stayed with the pack instead of coming with me. At least you would have learned how to fight."

"Fight? You mean, learn how to take a beating, right?" Landon snapped. "Did you actually think things got easier on me when you left? I was everyone's target. The only thing I learned how to do was to stay the hell out of the way. When Mom gave me a camera for my fourteenth birthday, it was an escape. It got me away from the pack during the day. At least at night, I could hide in my room."

Sawyer slammed on the brakes, almost getting rear-ended by the truck in back, resulting in a sharp blast from the driver's horn.

"Why is this the first I'm hearing all of this? You never said a word about any of it."

"What good would it have done?" Landon said with resignation. "It wasn't going to change anything. I was just grateful you came back for me."

"Shit. I had no idea they would've taken it out on you."

"It wasn't you... it wasn't me... they treated everyone like that. The stronger ones were already with them. It was the weaker ones they picked on, no one was spared."

"I was a fool not to have seen it. I'm sorry... I should've..."

"Should've what? Taken on a kid when you could barely take care of yourself? Man, this isn't your fault. I never blamed you for any of it. It's simply the way it was. Period."

"Perhaps. Doesn't make it any better," Sawyer muttered.

"I'm sorry I even brought it up. Our mate has been kidnapped by a freakin' bear and I'm scared we're going to lose her. I was starting to feel like we'd finally found a home, then this happens."

"On that one, we're on the same page. It's amazing how much our lives have changed by one stubborn and breathtakingly beautiful female."

"Yeah, she's amazing."

Sawyer focused on the truck ahead but could feel his brother's gaze on him.

"What?"

"We're gonna find her, right?"

"Yeah, Landon, we're gonna find her, and we're going to be together again. I promise."

Jace's truck made a right-hand turn off the highway, and Sawyer followed suit, headlights cutting through trees on either side of a well-worn road. The path led deeper into the woods until the small caravan came to a stop in front of a large building surrounded by cabins and smaller homes. People milled about, gathering together as the trucks approached.

Double doors opened on the larger building and light spilled out, showing a cavernous room filled with chairs. Jace strode toward the opening with everyone following him inside.

"Guess we better join them. Seems like the Alpha stirred the pack before we got here," Sawyer observed.

"I'm not getting left out of this," Landon said, a mulish set to his handsome face. "She's *our* mate."

"Sawyer, Landon, step up here so I can introduce you to the pack," Jace called out as they entered the building. "Before we get started, I want everyone to meet Sawyer Billings and Landon Monroe. They are Nova's Fated Mates and have already claimed her. I was hoping the introduction to the pack would have been more of a celebration, but it seems other plans have been set in motion."

Jace scrubbed his face and gratefully accepted a mug of something hot from one of the females.

"About a month ago, the grizzly shifter, Baron Cooper, approached me about an alliance and to mate with Nova."

Angry mutterings rose from the crowd, and Jace held a hand up, asking for silence.

Landon leaned closer to Sawyer.

"Cover for me. I need to run into town. I'll be back as soon as I can."

"What do you need from town? Everything is closed at this time of night," Sawyer protested.

"Trust me. I know what I'm doing."

With those words, Landon slipped from the hall, unnoticed by the pack who were fixated on their Alpha and what he was saying.

"I turned him down and foolishly thought that was the end of it. This afternoon, he lured my daughter out on a fake emergency call and abducted her from the Coburn Ranch. Mrs. Coburn identified one of the males by the name of Fritz, and the barn had the stench of bears, so it wasn't rocket science to figure out who had taken her."

The Alpha considered the crowd before him.

"I need your help to get Nova back. We're going up against grizzlies, and they're lethal in their bear form. Their sleuth isn't large, but it's going to take all of us to take them on."

"They feel bullets same as we do," someone from the crowd cried out. "Let's mix it up, give 'em hell with fangs and guns."

"That's what I'm talking about," another yelled.

Within seconds, the crowd was on their feet, stirred and ready to take on anything getting in their way.

Jace gave a satisfied smile and nodded.

"Thank you. Now, here's what we're gonna do."

The room fell quiet.

Nova was escorted outside and led down a barely perceptible trail behind the house. Surrounded by trees and scrubs, she wondered what they had in store for her. Had Cooper changed his mind and ordered to have her killed? The thought of dying before she'd truly lived tore at her. She'd just met her Fated Mates. They hadn't had a chance to enjoy their lives together yet. Was it already over?

One of the guards walked ahead, stopping at a patch of ground recently cleared away. She could barely make out the iron ring on a trap door, even with her enhanced vision. Opening the hatch, a soft light glowed from the opening and the shifter next to her pushed her toward it.

"Time to get settled in your new home."

Surprisingly, her escorts helped her down the steep steps, then unlocked her cuffs. Nova's shoulders ached from the enforced restriction, and a groan escaped before she realized it.

"There's food, water, and a bathroom. You'll stay here till the Alpha says otherwise. Don't get any ideas of escape, there's only one way out and the door is magically fortified with silver."

Nova gave the shifter a sidelong glance as she rubbed her wrists.

"Like the trap you set in the woods?"

The other guard barked a guttural laugh.

"Something like that. Got a few of them set out there. Boss figured it could cut the wolf pack numbers down… less to deal with, but none of them were laid out by your place. He didn't want you accidentally finding one. Now, be a good little pup and behave."

Their laughter echoed as the doors slammed shut, and the sounds of chains dragging across the opening ensured she was locked in.

Turning, Nova inspected her surroundings—a cot with folded sheets and blankets on it stood against the back wall, a small table and chair sat nearby, and a cubicle with only a toilet and basin was in the corner. A case of water lay on the floor next to the table with a small bag on top. Opening the bag, she discovered a wrapped sandwich and protein bars. Sniffing at the sandwich, she detected nothing out of the ordinary and hungrily wolfed it down. She had no idea how long she would be here, and her last meal had been the night before. Nova might be a lot of things, but stupid wasn't one of them.

Munching on a protein bar, she carefully scrutinized the walls for any weaknesses. Going by the structure and location, she was in a fortified cellar, so even if she were to find an opening, she'd still be trapped underground. The likelihood of escape was getting dimmer as time went by.

Nova grabbed a blanket, wrapping it around her shoulders, and sat on the cot, leaning against the wall. A slight breeze wafted across her face, and she looked up to see a vent above her head. The hum of a motor told her air was being filtered in by a generator, which warned her that her life was dependent on that piece of machinery. Without air, she wouldn't last very long down here.

She eyed the vent long and hard. The opening wasn't big enough for her, but her wolf could manage it. The problem was getting inside the vent, then shifting. It would take timing and agility. Pushing the table under the vent and climbing on top, she figured she'd give it a shot. It wasn't like she had anything else to do.

15

Sawyer sat at the long table beside Jace, his Beta, and several others of the pack. They were listening intently to a conversation on speakerphone.

"The shifter's name is Baron Cooper. He's Alpha to the grizzlies farther up the mountain."

"I know of him. Rodin Walker is in his employ."

"What do you know of this Walker fellow?"

"He's a pompous and over-bearing mage with a talent for metalworking. I can see where the two would gravitate toward each other. In your favor, however, his practical magic is at the level of parlor tricks."

"So, he's not a threat?"

"Even a fool can be a threat if they're lucky enough, Alpha." Miriam Bishop's chuckle was low and wicked. "Let me come with you tonight. I'm at loose ends and could use some entertainment."

"Thank you, Miriam." Jace sat back, a satisfied grin replacing the scowl. "Your help is always appreciated."

"We're taking the witch?" One of the older shifters asked after Jace had disconnected the call.

"We are. She's proven very helpful in the past, and I have a feeling we'll have need of her bag of tricks to infiltrate Cooper's settlement."

A whirl of light and color flashed onto the floor and settled into the form of Miriam Bishop. A long braid hung down her back, and a floor-length cape covered her leather-clad body and knee-high boots.

"You will, indeed, require my bag of tricks, as you so quaintly put it," the witch smirked. "It wouldn't do any good to storm up the mountain and have everyone hear us coming. Show me which vehicles you plan on using and I'll place a silencing spell on them. No one will hear us approach."

"That'll be handy," one of the shifters muttered.

Miriam arched a brow, a smug look on her face.

Jace stood, glancing around the table.

"Six trucks should hold everyone. Can you handle that many?"

"I can. Show me which ones."

"Troy, line up the trucks so Ms. Bishop can work her magic," Jace ordered. "Sawyer, I want you and... where's Landon, anyway?"

"Right here," Landon said, sprinting toward them. "I had to take care of something."

"Good enough," Jace nodded. "As I was saying, once we get there, you two should be able to locate Nova with your mate bond."

True to her word, the line of vehicles eased up the road in total silence. Sawyer rolled the window and listened to the quiet. The running engines didn't make a sound, no parts squeaked when they hit a pothole, nothing—only the wind howling through the night air.

"How long will it take to get there?" Landon asked from the back seat.

"About thirty minutes, give or take," Jace replied. "There's a spot a couple of miles before we get there where we're going to split up and circle Cooper's settlement. The pack is going to shift and cause a big enough distraction for us to get to Baron and Nova."

"Do you know where he's keeping her?" Sawyer asked.

"I don't, but I know which house belongs to the Alpha. I'm depending on you two to lead us to Nova. Once we get there, open your mate bonds. You'll be able to feel her and know if she's close or not."

"Good to know. We weren't quite sure how the bond worked in situations like this."

"It's a lot more powerful than the pack link, but distance plays an important factor. Naturally, the closer you are to each other, the stronger the connection."

It wasn't much longer before the line of trucks split off, half continuing straight while the other three veered off onto a road skirting the forest.

Sawyer kept testing his mate bond, trying to get a fix on Nova. A few moments later, familiar tendrils of emotion wrapped around him.

"I can feel Nova!"

"Is she all right?"

Even in the dark, Sawyer could make out the strain and worry on the Alpha's face.

"I can't really tell. It's hard to pin it down." Sawyer glanced at Landon. "What about you? Got anything?"

"Not much… I can feel her, but that's about it."

"Troy, make sure everyone is on the same channel with those walkie-talkies and in place. We need to find Nova and get out of there as quickly as possible."

"On it, boss."

"Alpha."

"Yes, Miriam?"

The witch had been silent the entire trip, and Sawyer had almost forgotten she was with them.

"I'm sensing the mage, and he's very excited. He's planning something."

"That's the last thing we need. Any idea what he's up to?"

"Not yet. I don't want to push too hard, or he'll figure out what I'm doing. I need him to visualize, then I should be able to see it." Beads of sweat formed on the witch's forehead as she concentrated. Sitting between Landon and Sawyer, they watched her in silence.

A howl of pain cut through the night air, and everyone froze.

"Traps. He set traps on the perimeter of the settlement," Miriam's words rushed out.

Troy murmured into the walkie-talkie and soon got a harried response.

"It's Eddie. He stepped in a trap. The others are loading him into the truck."

"Fuck! Make sure everyone is aware and to watch their step." Jace growled his frustration. "I'm going to skin that bear before this night is over."

Landon opened the case he'd been carrying since he returned from his errand.

"What's in there?" Sawyer asked.

"Tranq guns." Landon grinned. "I saw them in Nova's clinic earlier and figured we could use them. Got enough darts to take down a couple of bears, figured we'd go after this Baron character with them."

"Hell, yeah! Give me one of those," Sawyer crowed. "Time to hunt some bear."

Nova cursed as she ripped a nail, trying to pry the vent cover off. Straining with all her enhanced strength, she got a good enough grip and yanked hard. The table shot out from under her, and she fell with a crash, still holding the metal cover. All the air in her lungs was sucked out on impact, and Nova groaned as she haltingly got back to her feet. Inspecting the small table, she was relieved to discover it hadn't broken, only flipped over when she'd lost her balance.

Pushing the table back against the wall, she placed the chair on top as an added step to get into the vent. Not only was the climb precarious, but she was also going to have to squeeze into the small vent enough to shift and pray her wolf could take it from there. Shedding her clothes, she glanced back at the pile with regret. Nova would have to remain in wolf form or take the chance of freezing. She had no idea where the vent led or even if she could escape once she got to the end, but it was her only option, and she was taking it.

It was now or never. Taking a deep breath, Nova carefully climbed onto the table, then perched on the chair, moving as cautiously as possible. This close to the opening, it looked even smaller, and Nova frantically wondered if she could even get her shoulders through. There was only one way to find out. With a leap and a dive, she squirmed her arms, head, and shoulders into the narrow vent. Inching her way in as much as possible, she shifted... and prayed. Her wolf whined at the tight confines but crept forward, claws clacking on the metal surface. She had no way of knowing how far she'd crawled when she came upon a crosspiece. It would be a tight turn either way and she wasn't sure whether to go left or right until a faint breeze wafted in from her left. Taking it as a sign, she crawled in the direction of fresh air.

Another ten feet of ductwork and she found herself at the end of the road. The air she'd felt was coming from a tear in the seam of galvanized steel. Pushing against the opening with her paws, Nova managed to bend the metal, making the hole slightly larger. With renewed vigor, she pushed and strained against the duct until her paws and head fit through. Looking around, she found herself surrounded by trees. Deeming it safe, she kept digging her way through until she was free from the confines of the ductwork.

Panting from her exertion and leaving behind more fur than what she cared for on the ragged pieces of steel, she shook herself off and looked around to get her bearings. Nova looked down on Baron's home and the small encampment. Floodlights filled the area, and several people rushed around. The sounds of rifles being fired stopped her in her tracks as she tried to figure out what was happening. Then she saw them—wolves bounding from the woods, heading toward the houses. Her pack had shown up to rescue her, which meant her father and mates were somewhere around here, and she needed to find them… fast.

16

Opening his mate bond, Landon immediately felt Nova. She was alive and unharmed, but he couldn't pick up more than that. Relaying what information he had to Jace, the Alpha directed him and Sawyer to find her while he and the others concentrated on Baron Cooper and the bear shifters.

"You're going to need this more than me," Landon told Jace as he gave him the tranq gun.

"Hang on to the other one, just in case," Jace acknowledged with a tight smile. "Find my daughter… at all costs."

The Alpha didn't need to say it twice. There was no way in hell he and Sawyer were leaving this piece of mountain without her.

"She's not in the house," Sawyer pulled Landon off to the side. "But she's close."

"Yeah, getting that, too," Landon added. "But where?"

"Let's check out the back of the house."

Landon followed his brother as they canvassed the area, looking for anything which could lead them to their mate.

"Look over there!" Landon called out. "It's a path, and it looks like someone's used it recently."

"Might be what we're looking for," Sawyer agreed.

Gunfire, the roar of bears, and men yelling had Landon looking over his shoulder every few seconds. The place was fast turning into a battlefield, and he was ill-equipped to deal with it. He'd spent his life avoiding trouble, and now, he was smack dab in the middle of it. Nova's life was on the line, and she was his Fated Mate. It was time to grow a set and be the male she needed. He'd be damned if he would let her and Sawyer down.

Landon tore off down the path, Sawyer's warnings ringing unheeded in the air. He needed to find Nova. The path, bare of snow, was littered with boot-prints, which meant someone had been here not long ago.

"I found something!" He rang out triumphantly, spotting chains on the ground. Falling upon them, he let out a frustrated groan and then a yelp of pain when he realized the chains wrapped around the opening of a trap door and locked shut were silver laden. *What now?*

"Landon, behind you!"

He turned only to see a huge paw coming at him, batting him aside as if he were nothing more than a nuisance. Landon flew across the clearing, landing against the trunk of a tree. Shaking his head to clear it, he looked up to see Sawyer in his wolf form lunging at a towering grizzly bear. The beast had to be at least ten feet tall, and his brother was no match for it. Shifting, he scrambled to his paws and leapt for the bear's back, sinking his fangs deep into the beast's neck.

The bear swatted Sawyer through the air, and he yelped when he hit the ground hard. The glint of metal caught Landon's eye, and he recognized the tranq gun near his brother's fallen body. Opening his bond, he called out to Sawyer.

The gun is right next to you. Shift, Sawyer!

The bear roared in rage and shook Landon off like a bothersome flea. The bear headed toward Sawyer, and Landon attacked again, this time dodging in and around the animal's paws, hoping to trip him up.

Sawyer stirred and shifted, grabbing the gun and rising to one knee. He fired... once, twice. Still, the bear fought, then stumbled, and Landon darted out of the way. Sawyer fired a third round, and the bear crashed to the ground, shaking the surrounding trees, snow falling from the laden branches, covering them in a blanket of white and ice.

"Are you all right?" Landon shifted and hurried to Sawyer's side.

"Yeah, I'll live. Show me what you found," Sawyer said as he picked up his scattered clothing off the ground.

"There's a cellar door, but it's chained, locked, and full of silver."

Sawyer picked up the chain with a gloved hand and studied the lock.

"They're both in good shape, it's gonna be hard to break these, but the iron ring might give easier. If we do this together, we can get it."

Each grabbing a side of the chain, they pulled with all their might. The ring gave a bit, encouraging them to try harder. Working in tandem, they pulled until the ring flew free of the door, sending them both flying backward.

Scrambling on their knees, they went back to the door and tore it open. Landon climbed down the steps with Sawyer right behind him. They spun around in confusion finding the room empty.

"Where is she?" Sawyer growled. "Her scent is all over the place."

"She must have shifted," pointing at the pile of clothes on the floor. Seeing the table, chair, and open vent left the only conclusion. "She escaped through the vent."

"We need to find her. She doesn't know about the traps they set out around this place," Sawyer rasped.

That familiar feeling lodged in Landon's chest. The one he always got when he was searching for something.

"This way. Come on."

Tearing up the steps, Landon took off for the woods. He didn't wait for Sawyer and didn't look back. The mate bond and the sixth sense he had for finding things were working overtime, and he had to push on. He knew he'd find her.

Sounds of fighting faded into the background as Landon crashed through the woods. The only thing he heard was his own heavy breathing and curses as he dodged trees and bushes. It was like an invisible force was pulling him, and he had no choice but to follow. Nova was close... he was almost there.

"Nova! It's Landon. Where are you?"

He stopped for a moment and listened but heard no answer. Continuing on, he tried again.

"Nova!"

Faintly, off in the distance, he heard a voice. Landon stopped, leaning against a tree, trying to pinpoint which direction it had come from.

"Nova? Is that you?"

"Landon?"

It was all he needed. Sprinting through the trees, he raced toward her voice. She was up ahead, she was alive, and soon, she would be safe. They would all be together again, and they could put this nightmare behind them.

Nova let out a heavy sigh of relief. Landon was close. Moments later, she could hear him approaching and she ran to meet him.

"Landon! I'm here." She barreled into him, knocking him off balance, and they fell onto the ground in each other's arms, laughing and crying at the same time.

"Are you all right? Are you hurt?" Landon searched her for wounds or injuries.

"A few scratches and bruises. I'll be fine." She kissed him hungrily, thrilled to be with one of her mates again. "How did you find me?"

"The mate bond, though it wasn't as helpful as I'd thought it would be. Sawyer and I were able to find the cellar—"

"Where is Sawyer?" Nova searched for her other mate.

Landon looked confused. He tore off his coat and wrapped it around Nova, who stood shivering in the cold.

"He was right behind me." He threw his head back and groaned. "I've got to go back. Something must have happened to him."

"We'll go together," Nova told him. "We'll find him."

"No, you need to stay safe. I can't let you go back there."

"We're in this together. We need to find Sawyer, then we'll work on getting out of this mess. Here, take your coat. My wolf will be fine, and I can travel faster that way."

Together, they raced through the woods back toward the house and cellar, Nova bounding ahead with Landon close behind. She skidded to a stop upon seeing a gigantic bear sleeping on the ground near the cellar door.

"What happened to him?" she asked after shifting back, cautiously walking around the unconscious giant.

"I borrowed your tranq guns. You'll have to order some more darts. Pretty sure we used them all."

"Best purchase ever." Nova snorted. "Stay up here and keep watch. My clothes are in there, and I want them back.

"Be careful."

Nova cautiously entered the cellar. She didn't particularly want to go back down there, but weighing Wyoming's winter against traipsing around in the nude outside was a no-brainer, and retrieving her clothes won. She scented both mates in the small area, but no sign of Sawyer or anyone else was there. Grabbing her clothes, she speedily dressed and sprinted up the steps to rejoin Landon. She found him searching the area for tracks.

"Any sign of Sawyer?"

"No. My guess is someone grabbed him. There's no way he would've left us behind."

"Can you feel our link to him?" A cold dread tightened around Nova's heart, and it suddenly became hard to breathe. "I can't feel him, Landon. Please tell me he's still with us."

"He's not dead, Nova... he's just... not here." Landon pulled his cap off and raked his hair with his fingers. "When we got here, Sawyer and I both could feel your link, and it led us to the cellar, but I'm not getting anything from him now."

"Me, either," Nova said softly. "We need to find my dad and let him know what's going on."

"Come on. His truck is parked over there. I don't hear any more sounds of fighting, so they should be waiting for us."

Skirting around the house, Nova and Landon carefully made their way to where her father should have been waiting for them. Nova didn't see any of Cooper's sleuth, but she also didn't see any of her pack either. It was strangely quiet in the grizzly settlement.

"Something's not right, Landon. It's too quiet."

"I was getting that feeling myself," he agreed.

"Did Dad have a plan?"

"Other than get you and get out—no, that was it. He sent me and Sawyer after you while he dealt with the bear Alpha."

"It doesn't make sense."

"The trucks are over there. The others are on the other side of the settlement," Landon pointed out. He captured Nova's hand, and they walked together toward the vehicles.

"There's no one here."

Landon tugged on her hand to stop.

"Don't you have a link to the pack or your dad?"

"Yeah, but I'm getting nothing. It's the same as when I tried to feel Sawyer's bond."

"Magical interference, possibly?"

"I didn't think of that." Nova's eyes widened.

"Miriam Bishop is here with us. She said Cooper had his own mage too."

"It still doesn't explain where everyone is," Nova said, frustration getting the best of her. "Let's go back to Baron's house and see if anyone is there. There's no way everyone could've simply upped and disappeared."

"Give me a sec." Landon jumped in the back of Jace's truck and rummaged through a couple of boxes.

"What are you looking for?"

"These!" He held up two handguns and boxes of ammo. "We're not going back in unarmed."

17

"Wait! The traps!"

Sawyer let out a string of curses as he charged after Landon. The last thing he needed was for his brother to get caught in one of those damned silver-laden teeth again. The consequences would be so much worse this time around. They were Fated Mates, and the link bound them in ways they didn't begin to understand. He'd heard tales of what happened when one mate died, leaving behind a hollow shell of a mate... if they even survived the loss.

All of a sudden, Sawyer hit a wall of nothing and couldn't move. He strained with everything he had but couldn't move so much as a finger. *What the fuck was going on?*

"Two down!"

The laughter dripped with self-righteous smugness.

"Fighting is useless. You might as well conserve your energy."

A figure walked into Sawyer's line of vision. A man with a prominent widows peak, shoulder-length black hair and goatee, dressed in leather with a black cloak ending at mid-calf.

Black and leather must be a signature witch thing.

"Once I have you secured, I can focus on the other mate and finally collect what's owed me."

The mage waved his arms, and Sawyer spun in place, a web of nothingness holding him tightly bound. He floated in the air as Rodin walked beside him, carrying on a cheery conversation with himself. Instead of heading back toward the house, the mage went the other way, deeper into the forest, toward the mountains.

Minutes later, Sawyer was in a cave, being led down a narrow tunnel farther into the depths of the mountain. Entering an alcove, the mage lifted a hand, and Sawyer was laid on a worn-out sleeping bag.

Chanting softly under his breath, Rodin waved his arms at the opening of the small recess, then directed his focus on Sawyer.

"I've released you, but you're contained here. Stay and be a good dog. I have to find the other mate, so you won't be alone for long."

Sawyer felt when the bonds released, and he grunted as he got to his knees. As the mage had warned, there was an impenetrable barrier over the opening, so there was nothing to do but sit and stew.

He opened his mate bond, but there was nothing. It must be the magic messing with his link to Nova and Landon. If he was being kept alive, common sense told him the same would hold true for his mates. He hoped with everything in him that Landon had found Nova and they'd escaped, but in his heart, he knew better. Landon would never leave him behind. He'd search for him… and get captured, or worse, in the end.

Jace motioned to Bryce and Linc to go around to the back of the house while Troy and Miriam followed him. The rest of the pack would keep the sleuth busy while his group focused on Cooper and the mage. Hopefully, Sawyer and Landon would find Nova and get her out quickly. That was the plan, but he knew things could go sideways with little effort.

The front door swung open under Jace's hand on the doorknob, and he heard the voice before he saw him.

"Come on in, Alpha Adkins. I've been expecting you."

Jace eased inside the house to find Baron Cooper leaning against the fireplace mantel with a drink in one hand and Rodin Walker sitting in a nearby leather chair, a smug grin firmly in place.

"Where's my daughter?"

"Nova?" Cooper barked a short laugh. "She's perfectly safe. I've got her tucked away until I'm ready for her."

"She's already mated. Let her go!"

"Oh, please. Did you really think that would get in my way?" Baron walked toward the bar in the corner of the room and looked questioningly at Jace. "Care for a drink? No? No matter." He calmly poured another drink and took a sip. "You see, I was being nice when I asked for Nova to be my mate. I don't make a habit of asking for what I want. I take."

"She'll never accept you, and her mates will kill you for what you've done."

"That's where you're wrong. Once her mates are out of the way, those marks will fade, and I'll replace them with mine. She'll have no choice but to accept me, and that will open the way for me to further my plans along."

"What plans would those be?" There was no way in hell he would let this maniac get his way, but he had the upper hand at the moment, and Jace had to bide his time.

"Why, to be king of the hill, of course." Baron's eyes glowed golden and his canines extended. "I'm going to be the ruling Alpha of the Bighorn Mountains. All shifters will look to me for leadership, and I will have ultimate power over all shifters."

"That's a rather grandiose plan you have there," Jace said matter-of-factly.

"Some may think so, but it's been a long time in coming. My sleuth and I have been searching for a place to call home for quite a number of years. Since we've settled here, I realized I can make this a permanent home for my people."

"It's a big mountain, Cooper. We've shared it with others for centuries."

"Bears don't like to share, and we don't play well with others."

"Then why the need for my daughter?" Jace asked.

"A valuable asset. She's well-liked and because of her occupation, she's very useful. I can make use of that. Of course, I'll mate with one of my own for progeny. It wouldn't do for me to have hybrids running around."

Jace gave a short nod, and Bryce and Linc rushed Cooper, tackling him to the floor. Miriam stepped out and with a quick spell, froze the bear shifter in place. Troy headed for the mage, but the male was deceptively quick and lashed out with a power blast of his own, sending the Beta crashing across the room and into a wall, the impact shaking the entire house.

Baron's eyes glowed gold and despite the magical binding, he shifted and rose with a roar. With calculated swipes, he took out the enforcers, leaving them on the floor in a heap. Rodin touched Baron's arm and in a flash of light, they vanished from the room.

"What the hell?" Jace met Miriam's gaze, who appeared as shocked as he was.

"My apologies, Alpha, I severely underestimated the mage."

"It seems we both did." He eyed his men groggily getting to their feet. "Let's regroup and come up with a different plan."

As they walked the short distance to the trucks, Jace turned on his walkie-talkie.

"I want everyone to pull out and return home. No argument, no discussion, just do it."

"What are you doing?" Troy's brow lifted in surprise. "We can't take these bears on by ourselves."

"Which is why we need to come up with another plan. I'm not taking a chance on the pack getting wiped out by a bunch of grizzlies and a mage with more power than we realized." He grunted as he surveyed the houses below. "It's bad enough I haven't heard from Sawyer or Landon. I have no idea if they found Nova. This is all going to hell in a handbasket, and I don't like it one bit."

"Since there are only the five of us now, I can cloak us with a spell. We can walk around unseen and if we don't get too close to the mage, we can remain undetected," Miriam offered.

"That has some merit," Jace said thoughtfully. "I only wish I knew where to look. Guess we're going to have to do this the old-fashioned way. Troy, I want you, Bryce, and Linc to shift and do a little tracking. See if you can find Nova or her mates' scents. They have to be around here somewhere."

"What are you going to do?" Troy asked. "I should stay with you in case you need help."

"I'll be fine. Miriam will be with me. I'm sure we can handle anything that comes our way. Remember what she said though. Avoid the mage." He turned toward the witch. "Do your thing, Ms. Bishop. We need to find my daughter and her mates."

Miriam chanted a spell, then touched each of them in turn, vanishing from sight. Jace frowned.

"Alpha? Is something wrong?"

"I can't sense them. The pack link isn't working."

"The spell cloaks all aspects of the person and is only detectable to other magic users. Would you like me to take it off?"

"No, leave it." Jace shook his head as he mentally went through the pros and cons. "One sharp bark ought to be enough to signal the rest of us."

He glanced at Miriam who shook her head.

"They've gone."

"Looks like it's you and me. Let's see what we can find." Jace offered his arm, and the witch took it, as they walked toward the houses.

They searched every house they came across, only to find each one deserted. No Baron Cooper, no mage, and no bear shifters. It made no sense. Where could they have all gone? Where were Nova and her mates? He hadn't found their scents in any of the houses and didn't know where else to look.

Jace stepped outside the last home to find Miriam in the small yard staring off into the distance.

"Do you see something?"

"No, but I was thinking... wouldn't a bear shifter be just as comfortable in a cave?"

“Why the hell didn’t I think of that?” Jace could have kicked himself. It was so obvious, and he’d totally missed it. Where better for a group of bears to hide?

“The mountains are practically in Cooper’s back yard. We can walk there in a few minutes,” Miriam noted.

“Did I mention how much I appreciate you?” Jace asked with a rakish grin.

“Not today, but there’s still time.” Miriam winked and took off toward the mountains.

18

"What do you mean she's not there?" Baron Cooper roared.

"It looks like she got out by the vent."

"The vent?" Baron narrowed his eyes at the male. "There's no way in hell she could've fit through that small of an opening."

"It's the only way out, sir, and the cover was off with a table and chair propped against the wall." The speaker flinched, waiting for the blow he knew was to come. "It had to be her wolf, sir."

"And I suppose her wolf can fly?" He shoved the male down, striding toward the entrance of the cave. "It seems Ms. Adkins is creative as well as flexible." He whirled around, facing his men. "Find the bitch and be quick about it. We still need her other mate."

The cavern emptied, leaving Baron and Rodin alone.

"Is the prisoner secure?" Baron spat, turning on the mage.

"Of course, Alpha," Walker acknowledged with a small bow.

"Make sure! This is getting complicated, and I don't have time for it. I want those males out of the way, and I want Nova under my thumb. I can't proceed until it's done."

"I'll see to it right away."

Baron paced the hard ground, muttering to himself.

"Why do you persist?"

The bear shifter stopped short, glaring at his sister.

"Why do you think, Lorena? We need a home."

"We had a home, Baron, a good one."

"You call that good?" He snorted in derision. "As I recall, we were exiled."

"Whose fault was that?" Lorena spoke softly.

"The council was stuck in the stone age. They refused to listen to reason..."

"They refused to listen to an arrogant cub who threatened their way of life."

"Be careful, sister, you go too far."

"I don't go far enough, brother," she spat. "Why can't you ever be satisfied? Why do you always have to have more? The world doesn't owe you anything."

"Which is why I take what I want," he roared. "This mountain is going to be mine! My sleuth will have a home free of oppression and backward thinking."

"Pay attention, Baron. You're losing your sleuth. This war you've started with the wolves is one you can't win. Open your eyes. The bears are already leaving you. They would rather ask forgiveness from the Council than stay here under your leadership."

"You lie!"

"Do I? Maybe if you'd listen to anyone other than your mage, you'd realize the truth."

"Leave! I don't have time for this."

For a moment, regret filled Baron when Lorena left the cavern. At one time, they'd been close. He'd trusted her with his dreams and ambitions, but though she still followed him, she didn't support him as she once did. No matter. He had more important things to attend to. He would deal with his sister later.

Nova held Landon's hand tightly as they made their way back to the bear shifter's compound. She wasn't taking any chances on losing this mate as well. She'd come to the realization of how important both males had become to her, how much she needed both of them in her life. Sawyer and Landon were woven into her life now in a way which couldn't be separated. They were her mates, and she loved them both.

"It's going to be all right," Landon said softly.

"Do you sense something? Do you know where Sawyer is?" Nova stopped short, pulling Landon to stand beside her.

She'd learned a long time ago how to mask her feelings, but that didn't come into play between Fated Mates. Landon flinched when he saw the pain etched on her face, raw and anguished. There was nothing she could do about it. They'd been through so much together in such a short time. They'd met in adversity and were still going through it. She didn't know what Fate had in store for them, but she'd welcome a break of any kind at this point.

"Sorry, no, I'm still in the dark. Believe me, if I had any idea where my brother was, I'd be there already." He gazed into her eyes, and she saw his pain. He loved his brother with the intensity of a shared life, something she couldn't match—yet.

Pulling her close, Landon kissed her deeply, his tongue tangling with hers, claiming her as his own. She didn't care that they were out in the open… easy targets. She needed the reassurance of his love and the hope they would find their other mate so they could be whole again.

Landon pulled away reluctantly, but held on to her hand, kissing it through the glove.

"I could happily spend a lifetime kissing you, but we need to find Sawyer." Landon's voice was raspy, and his attempt at a grin was off the mark. "Then, we'll have a lot of kissing… and more to make up for."

"Sounds like a plan," Nova agreed. "Any idea where to start looking?"

"Let's check out Cooper's house, if they're not there, maybe we can find a clue to where everyone is."

"It's as good a place to start as any. Let's go."

Nova took off at a brisk pace, Landon by her side. They didn't waste time talking or guessing at unknown possibilities. They had a goal and were focused on only one thing—find Sawyer.

Cautiously entering Baron's home, they found the place empty. Checking each room, they found no one. Nova walked into the Alpha's office and found Landon staring intently at a framed picture.

"Find something?"

"I'm not sure." Landon turned to face her. "Something is telling me this picture is important. Does it look familiar to you?"

Intrigued, Nova crossed the room and took the photo from him. It was a black-and-white photo of Baron Cooper, a young woman, and several other males in front of a large cave.

"This looks familiar..." Nova stared hard at the photo. "Wait, I know where this is. It's not far from here." She grabbed Landon's hand and took off, excitement coursing through her veins.

Why hadn't she thought of it before? She knew where Sawyer was.

Running through the forest, Nova and Landon didn't slow down until they could see the Bighorn mountains ahead.

"Baron's cave is up ahead," Nova pointed out.

"Tell me about this cave. What's so important about it?"

"I remember Dad telling me about it. When Baron and his sleuth first got here, they lived in the caves until they built homes for everyone. These caves are huge, and tunnels go for miles in the mountain."

"You're thinking they're in there and they have Sawyer?"

"That's precisely what I'm thinking," she said excitedly. "Odds are, Dad figured it out as well, and I bet they're here somewhere."

"You would be right, sweetheart."

"Dad!" Nova whirled around in excitement, only to stop in confusion when she didn't see her father. "Dad?"

Her father gradually materialized in front of her, a wicked grin on his face.

"What the..."

"Language, young lady."

"You're gonna play that card?" Nova hurled herself into her father's strong and welcoming arms. "We didn't know where you were." She forced herself to breathe. "Dad, they have Sawyer. We can't find him anywhere."

"It's all going to be okay. At least I know you and Landon are all right. We'll find Sawyer, I promise."

Nova noticed the witch, Miriam Bishop, standing off to the side.

"Oh, now things are making more sense"—Nova observed, putting the puzzle pieces together.

"Cooper's mage is a lot stronger than I realized, and we needed more stealth to find you and your mates before we tried to make a move again."

Something brushed against Nova's leg, and she looked down in surprise, only to see nothing around her. A low whine caught her attention.

"Who's that?"

Miriam chanted a phrase, waved her hand, and three wolves materialized in front of them. Troy padded to Jace and met his gaze. After a few moments, Jace turned to the rest of them.

"Looks like we were right. They have Sawyer. He's in an alcove, but there's a magical barrier preventing any escape. Baron is in there, but the mage was sent back to the compound to look for Nova and Landon. It seems most of the sleuth have deserted Cooper, returning to their former home."

"Sounds like the odds are leaning more in our favor," Landon noted.

"And I'm not one to argue with any kind of break," Jace agreed. "Miriam, can you take on the mage? We need to incapacitate him at all costs. The rest of us can take on Baron and what's left of his men, then we can get to Sawyer and call this a day."

"I've got this." Miriam nodded, determination stamped on her face. "I've had nothing but time to think about how to deal with that slimy bastard."

"Before we go, could you please cloak my men once again? They like the leverage of not being seen."

"I thought you wolves didn't care for magic?" Miriam laughed low.

"It's not our first choice, but I know an advantage when I see one, and right now, I will do anything to get my daughter's mate free from that narcissistic bastard."

"Point taken, Alpha," Miriam said with a smile, then chanted over the wolves once again.

Nova watched her father assemble the group. He'd argued about her joining the small party. He'd wanted her to wait for them in the forest, but one glance at her face and he'd given up with a heavy sigh. There was no way she would stay behind like a good little girl.

Landon pulled Nova aside, handing her his gun.

"Take this. I'll be able to help more if I shift." His gaze dropped to the ground. "At least my wolf can fight."

"Never doubt your strength or yourself, Landon." Nova palmed Landon's cheek and kissed him softly on the lips. "Not everyone is meant to be a warrior, but that doesn't mean you can't fight for those you love. I'm hardly a fighter either, but our mate is in there and we're going to get him out."

"Yeah, we are." His smile was a little crooked, and it melted Nova's heart. Her mates were both a little broken, but she knew deep in her heart her love would mend those cracks and make them whole again. She simply needed time.

Landon shifted and stood beside her as they joined her father and the rest.

The wolves entered the cave first, stationing themselves around the cavern until Nova and the others approached.

The musky odor of bears tickled Nova's nose as she entered the cave. She wondered how many were in there when the sound of roars and growls echoed in the chamber. The wolves had attacked, and there was no time for wondering.

Nova and Landon rushed in to find three bears in the cavern engaged with her father. The grizzlies were obviously confused as to what was going on because they could see only one wolf. Landon leapt into the fray at Jace's side, keeping them distracted. Nova inched her way along the wall, trying to get to the tunnel leading deeper inside the cave. Sawyer was back there—she only had to find him.

"Sawyer!" Nova hissed loudly. He was here... she knew it.

"Nova?" Sawyer's voice came back to her from farther down the tunnel.

She raced through the dark arches, focused on one thing only... getting to her mate.

Sawyer appeared in the opening of an alcove, and Nova skidded to a stop.

"What are you doing here? It's not safe." Sawyer anxiously looked past her.

"We're getting you out of here."

"You can't. The mage has some kind of magical barrier in place. I can't get out."

"There has to be a way." Nova ran her hands over the opening only to pull back sharply when she was zapped by the barrier.

"I'm sorry, but your mate is in there until the mage releases the spell."

Nova whirled around, gun in hand, to find a young woman blocking the tunnel entrance.

"Who are you?" Nova demanded.

"I'm Lorena, Baron's sister. I mean you no harm," she said softly, her hands raised. "I can help."

"Why would you want to help me?" Nova asked suspiciously. She'd had her fill of bear shifters in the last couple of days and wasn't about to start trusting one now.

"Because what my brother is doing is wrong. I've tried to tell him, but he won't listen to reason. So, I'm taking things into my own hands, then returning to our original home... if your pack will allow it."

"If you release Sawyer, I'll guarantee your safety. I can't say the same for your brother and his mage."

"He needs to be held accountable for his actions. Baron has had his way for far too long."

"So, how do we get my mate out of this?" Nova hitched a thumb at the invisible barrier separating her from Sawyer.

"Rodin's spell is the only thing that can bring it down." Lorena smiled slyly. "But I happen to know it."

She stepped forward and whispered a few words. Sawyer tentatively put a hand up and touched Lorena's shoulder.

"Sawyer!" Nova rushed up to him and hugged him for all she was worth, claiming his mouth with a soul-shattering kiss. "I was so scared I'd never find you."

"It's going to be all right. Where's Landon?"

"He's up front, fighting with Dad and the others."

"Come, we need to hurry before Rodin returns," Lorena urged.

19

Nova, Sawyer, and Lorena hurried toward the main cavern into the midst of roiling dust and the roars and growls of battling bears and wolves. Two bears lay dead on the ground, shifting back to their human form when death took them. Jace and Landon were doubling up on another bear while the cloaked wolves and Miriam dealt with Baron. Nova scanned the cave but saw no sign of the mage. It was only a matter of time before he appeared. She wasn't deluding herself on that score.

Sawyer shifted and before Nova could stop him, he'd jumped in beside Landon, sinking fangs deep into the bear's hide. Grizzlies were formidable opponents, and one wolf was rarely enough to take one down by itself.

The air suddenly charged with electricity, and Lorena grabbed Nova's arm, pulling her back against the cave wall.

"Rodin's here. He'll know immediately that the barrier is down. We need to hide."

"Hide, hell... that bastard needs to pay," Nova growled. Opening her bond link and mate link simultaneously, she let her mates and pack know the mage was there and to be aware, but it was Miriam she needed to get to with the information.

Sprinting across the cavern, she made a beeline for the witch, shouting to get her attention. As Miriam turned, a bolt of pure energy struck Nova in the back, knocking her to the ground. Howls of rage reverberated in the enclosure, a deafening din of rage, fear, and anguish. Dazed but still conscious, Nova crawled toward the witch. Thankfully, Miriam had seen enough and took matters into her own hands.

With a sweeping motion of her arms, the witch yelled out a spell, filling the air with a bright yellow light. Rolling it into a giant ball, she hurled it at the mage, who screamed in pain. Without giving him time to react, she shot huge bolts of magic at him, one after the other, until the mage crumpled to the ground. His body lit up from within, then disintegrated to dust before everyone's stunned gazes.

Baron lay on the ground in human form, bleeding, broken, and gasping his last breath. Jace stood over him, fangs ominously close to his throat, while

Landon and Sawyer rushed to Nova's side. Troy, Bryce, and Linc circled the bear shifter, watchful and waiting. There were no other bear shifters to deal with other than Lorena, who'd rushed to Nova when she fell.

Sawyer and Landon hovered over her, but Nova's pain was excruciating, and she couldn't bear to be touched. Her mates eased her coat off, then elongating their claws, tore away at her shirt. Her back was severely burned, bits of clothing sticking to the wound.

"Try to shift," Sawyer pleaded. "Your wolf can heal faster."

"I don't know if I can," she gasped. "So much pain..."

Landon clutched her hand like a lifeline.

"Please try."

Nova tried to draw in a deep breath, but the pain was too intense. Instead, she lay still, focusing on her wolf, bringing on the shift so she could begin to heal. In her head, it dragged on forever, but she finally felt the transformation take over. When she'd fully shifted, she let out a heavy sigh and passed out.

Sawyer gently picked up his unconscious mate, and Landon remained at his side. Jace and the others shifted, surrounding Baron. The shifter's sister was explaining her presence to the wolves.

"Jace!" Sawyer called out. "The woman helped Nova. She released me from my cell. Please allow her to return to her home as a favor to us."

The Alpha studied the young woman thoughtfully, then nodded.

"You may leave, but I can't say the same for your brother, I'm afraid."

"I understand," Lorena said quietly. "May I say goodbye to him?"

"Yes, but make it quick. He doesn't have much longer by the looks of it."

Lorena held Baron's hand and spoke quietly, then after a few moments, reached out to close his eyes. Rising, with tears in her eyes, she nodded to the group and left the cave.

"How's Nova?" Jace asked, approaching the pair of mates holding his daughter.

"She's sleeping. If it's all right with you, we'd like to get her home so she can rest more comfortably."

"Of course, Troy will take you all home. I have an injured male I need to check on, then I'll be by to make sure Nova's healing. Take care of yourselves."

Landon shook the Alpha's hand, and they made their way out of the cave, headed toward the vehicles. Following Troy, they jogged through the forest, only slowing down when Nova whimpered in pain. As one, Sawyer and Landon slowed to a walk until their mate calmed down, and only then did they pick up speed once again.

It was a slow, tedious process, but they finally reached the trucks. Once Sawyer was settled in the back with Nova, Landon rode shotgun, and Troy started the engine.

"I can't believe this nightmare is over," Landon groaned as he slumped in his seat. "All I want is for Nova to heal and have an absolutely boring few weeks of nothing going wrong."

Troy snorted, and Sawyer laughed.

"Right there with you, brother. I've had enough excitement to last me a lifetime."

"Come on, guys," Troy said. "The way I hear it, you two have been on the road for years with no pack, taking jobs in different cities. There has to be a ton of adventures you've had together."

Landon looked back at Sawyer, and they grinned at each other.

"Believe it or not, our lives have been kind of tame," Sawyer admitted.

"Living life under the radar," Landon added. "We didn't want to piss off any pack going through their territory, so we didn't make waves.

"Ah, got ya." Troy nodded in understanding. "Well, you're pack now, so I hope you two are planning on settling down here with Nova. As a rule, it's usually low key out here, but there are a few different shifters on Bighorn, so there's always a chance tempers are gonna flare once in a while."

"Sawyer and I found our home when we found Nova. We're not planning on leaving unless she wants to go somewhere." Landon said quietly.

"Yeah, she's settled here with the pack and her business in town. I know for a fact her parents are thrilled she's mated now. Better prepare yourself for being bombarded by a pair of anxious wannabe grandparents." Troy laughed heartily. "They've been wanting Nova to find a mate for years now, but Jace had promised Nova he would never push, letting her find someone she truly loved."

"She might've got more than she bargained for with us," Sawyer joked. "But she'll never lack for love. That's something she'll have in spades."

"Sounds like a good deal." Troy smiled at Landon and caught Sawyer's gaze in the rearview mirror. Pulling up to Nova's cabin, he added, "Here we are. I'll have someone drop your truck off in the morning. You got a way to get inside?"

"Yeah, I know where the spare key is. I'll get it and meet you at the door," Landon said as he hopped out the truck and headed for the garage.

Within minutes, they were inside, Troy had departed, and they were getting Nova settled in bed. Landon started a fire in the bedroom and downstairs while Sawyer covered Nova's silver wolf with a throw. He knew the wolf wouldn't be cold, but the need to do something for their mate was overwhelming.

Watching Nova sleep, Sawyer was overcome with so many emotions, some of them new to him—remorse, regret, anger, fear—They all roiled in him, threatening to break the composure he'd held together for so many years. He and Landon had just begun to enjoy their lives with their Fated Mate, and she'd been taken from them. That feeling of helplessness had almost done him in, and he vowed to be a better and stronger mate for Nova and Landon, one they could depend on in any given situation. He would do anything in his power to protect them, and if he had to become more hardened and stronger, then by the Goddess, he would!

Landon entered the bedroom bearing a tray covered with food, and Sawyer smiled at him gratefully.

"Thanks. To be honest, I can't remember the last time I ate." Clearing a spot on the dresser for the tray, he began piling food on a plate. "So much has happened I'm not real sure what day it even is."

"Right there with you, bro, but to be honest, I don't even care. I'm simply grateful to be back home with you and Nova."

"It truly is our home, isn't it?" Sawyer chewed thoughtfully as he watched Nova sleeping. "She took us in when we needed help and our whole world changed overnight."

"Can't say I ever want to go through stepping in a bear trap or getting silver poisoning again, but it brought us to our mate, and I'll always be grateful for that."

After they finished eating, Landon looked at Sawyer.

"What do we do now?"

"We rest and wait for Nova to wake. Don't know about you but my wolf wants to be near her."

"Sounds like a winner."

Together, they shifted and joined Nova on the bed, curling around her sleeping body. Sawyer's wolf chuffed happily, then settled down to sleep.

20

Nova woke but didn't open her eyes. The familiar warmth of her mates against her as she snuggled against them was comforting. She knew she was home, the scent of her bedroom was reassuring, and she was safe between Sawyer and Landon. She took stock of her injuries and felt no pain or burning, which made her wonder exactly how long she'd been asleep. Shifting, she touched her mates, rousing them from their slumber.

"Guys?" she said softly.

As one, Sawyer and Landon shifted beside her, curling around her until she was sandwiched between them from head to toe. Sawyer kissed her softly while Landon kissed her shoulder and caressed her breasts.

"I want to wake up like this every morning," Nova chuckled.

"We can make that happen," Landon husked in her ear.

Nova relinquished her dominance, letting Sawyer and Landon take over in the lovemaking. She responded to their touch, their kisses, their caresses... moving where they wanted her as they shared her body, giving her more pleasure than she ever knew existed. Strong hands squeezed and caressed her, while others traced the contours of her body. The stubble of Landon's unshaved jaw rasped against her tender inner thigh while Sawyer's soft beard nuzzled her neck. Sweat-dampened bodies covered hers and all she could do was gasp in pleasure as they teased and kissed her to dizzying heights of arousal.

When Sawyer pushed her knees up and wedged himself between her thighs, Landon coaxed her mouth around his shaft, which she took eagerly, licking and sucking as he growled with pleasure. The shared heat and sensations thrilled her. Sawyer's tongue was setting off a blinding heat inside her, and before she could find release, Landon plunged deep and hard inside of her, filling and stretching her with rough strokes. She cried out her pleasure, and Sawyer smothered her cries with a hot kiss filled with desire. They continued to share and switch, exploring every part of her body, leaving no expanse untouched. A wild orgasm ripped through her, then another. She was being loved thoroughly and completely, and her mind was dizzy from the incredible sensations coursing through her veins.

Landon pulled her on top of him and held her close as Sawyer slowly entered her from behind. Landon's lips crushed against hers as Sawyer pushed his way in, clasping her hips hard against him. When he was seated deep inside of her, Landon and Sawyer found their rhythm, passion burst where they were joined, and their bodies shuddered as they came with a shared release.

Unspoken, and in perfect harmony, Sawyer and Landon marked Nova again over their existing marks, claiming her together as Fated Mates. The mate bond flared open with an intensity that was nothing like the first time. This time, they shared everything—thoughts, hopes, dreams, feelings—and their links fused together, completing them as a true unit.

Spent and satiated, Nova lay between her mates. She'd almost dozed off again when she remembered something when she'd first woken.

"Guys?"

"Again?" Landon smirked.

"No... well, not yet anyway." She giggled and playfully smacked his leg. "I was wondering... how long have I been sleeping. My back is completely healed, and I feel fine."

Sawyer turned on his side to face her, caressing her cheek with his large hand.

"You've been out for two days."

"Two?"

"Yeah," Landon agreed. "Your dad checked on you the first night, then your parents came over the next day. They said to let you rest and call them when you were up and about."

"But my clinic!" Nova sat up with a start. "What day is it?"

"It's Friday, and the clinic is fine." Sawyer chuckled.

"I went to town and put a sign in the door and set up a voice message saying you were out for the week and would return to work on Monday. We've been checking your messages from here and everything is fine. No emergencies to worry about," Landon filled her in.

"Thanks for taking care of that." She slumped against the headboard in relief. "I owe the two of you big time."

"You owe us nothing."

"You're our mate," Landon said as his hand rubbed up and down her leg. "We'll always do what we can to take care of you."

"More so now, than ever," Sawyer agreed.

"What do you mean?" Nova looked at Sawyer curiously. His eyes were hooded from her, and she couldn't read them, but his emotions were all over the place.

"We've been doing a lot of thinking the past couple of days," Sawyer said haltingly, gathering his thoughts. "Being packless for so long, neither of us learned how to fight and defend. We've spoken to your father, and he's agreed to have Bryce and Linc train us."

"That's not necessary. I would never ask that of either of you."

"We know," Landon said. "It's something we feel we *need* to do."

"Hopefully, we'll never have a situation like this ever again, but we want to be prepared if it does," Sawyer added.

Before she could say anything else, Landon rushed on, his grin infectious and endearing. She couldn't help but smile back at him and reached for a stray lock on his forehead, pushing it back gently.

"I've got something else to tell you." He winked. "I've always toyed with the idea of opening a small gallery to sell my photos... get consignments from local artists, stuff like that. While I was in town, I saw an empty shop not far from your clinic. I called and spoke to the owner and made arrangements to rent the space."

Landon beamed at her, and she kissed him soundly as she hugged him tightly.

"That's wonderful news! Are you talking about the Franklin space?" When he nodded, she laughed delightedly. "It's a perfect place for a gallery, and we can have lunch together." She glanced over at Sawyer, who smiled back at her.

"I was thinking... if you didn't mind, I could convert one of the guest bedrooms into an office and I could work from home. Dinner would be on me during the week and Landon will cook on weekends...

and I can meet the two of you for lunch," Sawyer added.

"Guys, this is amazing." Nova looked at both of them, her eyes filling with tears. "I can't believe all this came together while I was sleeping." She reached out to touch them tenderly. "We're going to have the perfect life together. I love you both so very much."

"We're going to spend our lives showing you how much we love you," Sawyer kissed her gently on the lips.

Landon waited for the kiss to end before he reached for her, taking her into his arms to kiss her too.

"You're our Fated Mate, and you will always be the most important person in our lives."

Two weeks later

Nova entered the last of her notes into her laptop and closed the program down for the day. It had been busier than usual, everyone bringing in their animals to be vaccinated, and there had been a record number of adoptions from the local shelter. She sighed when the bell over the front door rang. Looking at the clock on the wall, she wondered who was coming in at almost closing time.

Heading to the front, she was surprised to see her father walk in.

"What brings you here?" She kissed him on the cheek as he wrapped her in a warm hug.

"Merely checking on my eldest," Jace said tenderly. "I wanted to make sure you and your mates were coming out to the full moon run tonight."

"We wouldn't miss it."

"Good. I want to introduce Sawyer and Landon to the pack officially and celebrate your mating. They're going to be an integral part of the pack, and I want it known from the beginning."

"I appreciate it, Dad, but we don't want any special favors."

"It's not, sweetheart. Those males have proven themselves and have the fortitude to better themselves in order to care for you. They've earned the right."

"Coming from you, that's saying a lot. Thank you."

"All I ever wanted was for you to be happy. You've got that now, and your mother and I couldn't be more pleased." Jace beamed at her.

"I'm happier than I ever imagined I could be. My life is almost perfect."

"Almost?" His question was hopeful.

"No pups yet, Dad." Nova laughed. "But it's not from Sawyer and Landon's lack of trying."

"Too much information, young lady."

Nova held her sides as she laughed again, and it felt good to be so happy.

"I love you, Dad."

"Love you too, sweetheart." Jace hugged her tightly. "Gotta run and pick up a few things for your mom from the store. We'll see all of you tonight."

"Count on it."

Nova watched her father leave then turned to close the clinic for the day. Her life was rich and full of love with two of the finest males to ever be blessed with. She was happy and knew that no matter what happened, she and her mates would always come through it together. Life was good.

The Triple Moon Trilogy
continues in book two...

Mystic Moon

Mystic Moon

Triple Moon Trilogy

Book 2

Reagan Adkins' entire life revolves around teaching... not only educating but helping the young people in her pack control their shifter abilities and acclimate them into a world of humans. Keeping busy means she doesn't have time to dwell on what she's lost.

Nash Collins spent the last fifteen years as a Navy Seal, dedicated to his country and brothers-in-arms, but he's never forgotten the love he left behind. Now, he's back home and trying to piece together the life he left, including Reagan. Winning her trust is proving to be far more difficult than he realized. It doesn't help that she's turned to another for the solace and comfort he longs to give her.

The love of a Fated Mate never dims, but losing trust in that person can drastically change the dynamics. Can he salvage the broken trust between them? Can Nash win Reagan's love all over again?

Before You Go!

If you liked this book, please do me a huge favor and leave a review. Reviews are a small thing that means so much to authors. They're invaluable as a means of advertising.

Leaving an Amazon review is like telling your friends you liked a book. After a book gets 20 reviews, Amazon suggests books in "also bought" and "you might like this" lists. This increases a book's visibility which boots sales.

After 50 to 75 reviews, Amazon highlights the book for spotlight positions for its newsletter. This is a HUGE boost for the author! Reviews help authors to sell more books.

An honest review is one of the most important things you can do to support an author. So, if you enjoyed this book, I'd be eternally grateful if you'd head over to Amazon, Goodreads, or BookBub and leave a review.

Thanks in advance!

Madison Granger
AUTHOR

Also By Madison Granger
Paranormal Romance

The Kindred Series
Phoenix Rising
Eternal Embrace
A Destiny Denied
Blindsided
Deuces Wild
Fated Journey
A Warrior's Redemption

Amelia
The Awakening of Amelia
The Rising of Amelia

Bayou Crescent Wolves
Zane

Stand-Alone
Save The Last Dance
Heart of Stone
A Valkyrie's Vow
Gambit
An Unexpected Legacy
Claiming Magick

Urban Fantasy

To Kill A Demon

PHOENIX RISING

Book One of The Kindred Series

Madison Granger

CHAPTER 1

Torie conceded to two thoughts simultaneously... Christmas shopping was overrated, and the spirit of Christmas was dead, buried under a glittering blanket of commercialism. She'd never been a big fan of crowds. There were way too many people out and about this weekend for her liking. She was doing her best to forge through the masses to get the last elusive gift items on her list.

Then there was the traffic.

Seriously! Did everyone think they had the only vehicle on the road?

It seemed the streaming multitude left their IQ's and common sense at home. If she made it to her house in one piece, she would consider herself a holiday shopper survivor.

Torie parked her SUV, sighing with resignation about the things she couldn't control. Grabbing her cell phone, keys, and purse, she headed across the full parking lot to the local bookstore. She'd been out all morning and most of the afternoon in search of Christmas presents for friends.

Usually, she shopped online, but sometimes you just had to get out and fight the crowds for that *perfect* gift. Unfortunately, those *perfect* gifts were getting harder and harder to find, or someone else had the same idea and by the time Torie got to the shelf, they were already gone. Frustration was rearing its ugly head. She'd come to the realization that she needed an indulgence break before continuing her search. A book for herself and a shot of caffeine should brace her for the rest of the shopping day.

Entering The Literal Word, she was regaled with bright lights, colorful displays, and Christmas music playing over the speakers. Torie loved this store. She delighted in the convenience of shopping online, but there was nothing like browsing aisles and shelves of books.

Here, she was in her element. Books were her comfort zone, her friend, and her solace when she needed mental pampering. As she glanced around the setup, Torie took in the crowd browsing for books or the latest book-related gadget, and there were plenty of them. People were running into each other trying to get through narrow passages to look at all the items.

Java Joe's, the in-house coffee shop, was also catering to a maximum crowd. Wistfully, Torie wondered if she would be able to get a cappuccino after she'd made her purchases. Slinging her bag up on her shoulder, she navigated to her favorite section.

A romance book with a sexy werewolf or vampire was always a welcome escape from her busy, but lonely life. An auburn-haired, green eyed, middle-aged divorcee, Torie was a graduate of the *been there, done that, have a drawer full of t-shirts* school of life. After more than her share of failed relationships, she was pretty sure the rest of her life was going to be spent alone. Being on the more-than-curvy side ensured it. Men her age seemed to all want that pretty, young trophy-type on their arm. *It is what it is* had become her mantra.

It wasn't a bad life, in itself. Torie had family, a brother and sister. She also had a grown daughter and a precocious granddaughter she adored. She had a job she liked, and made a decent living, too. There just wasn't a special man in her life. That kind of loneliness was hard for her. It had been a long time since there had been anyone memorable. Torie missed the best parts of a relationship, the companionship, sharing of ideas and thoughts, laughter, and the sex.

Yeah, I miss the sex.

Shaking her head ruefully, she berated herself for the pity party. That kind of thinking was depressing and never got her anywhere. It was time to shove it back into that tiny compartment in her brain and try, once again, to forget about it.

Approaching the paranormal romance section, Torie noticed they'd added a tier of shelves right before it of new releases.

Well, this makes it a little easier to find what I'm looking for.

Browsing through the titles, she scanned for releases by her favorite authors first. Torie picked up a few unknowns and started reading the back covers to find her next book boyfriend. After selecting a couple that seemed promising, she ambled over to another section of her favored genres, science fantasy. There was one book that had been released recently. She wondered if it was on the shelf yet, or if she would have to order it.

When she got to the section, Torie spotted her goal on the lower shelf.

Naturally! Why do they have to put them way down there?

Bending down, she grabbed the book. As she straightened, she lost her balance, dropping books and purse with a crash. Reddening with embarrassment, Torie bent down to retrieve her goods with a muttered oath. A man's strong, long-fingered hand came into her line of vision, reaching for her books as Torie grabbed her purse.

"Allow me," entreated an amused deep voice. He held her arm, lending her his support so she could stand.

Flustered beyond belief, still blushing furiously, Torie peered up to thank the man for his kindness. She gazed into the most mesmerizing pair of sky-blue eyes she'd ever seen. Torie found herself struck dumb. She took in his shaved head, and a handsome face with a sexy soul patch under his bottom lip, and a drop-dead killer smile.

"Tha... thank you." She finally managed to stammer.

"Always a pleasure to assist a lady in distress." He smiled back at her.

The handsome stranger held the books out to her. Regaining her composure, Torie reached up to take them. She couldn't help but notice how very tall he was. She looked up to give him a grateful smile.

His tailored slacks and button-down shirt did nothing to disguise the definition of a well-sculpted body. The rolled sleeves partially covered what appeared to be a full sleeve of tribal tattoos on his right arm.

Oh my, this guy is the stuff fantasies are made of.

His gaze went from her arms loaded with books to making eye contact.

"Have you found everything you were looking for?"

His smile, devastatingly sexy, sent her heart into overdrive. It'd been ages since she found herself attracted to any man, and here was the proverbial *sex on a stick,* talking to *her*. She said a quick prayer not to flub this.

"Yes, as far as shopping for books goes, I'm pretty well done."

"In that case," he started, his voice low and husky, "could I interest you in a coffee?"

Torie swallowed hard. He seemed sincere. There was no way she was going to pass up the chance to find out who this gorgeous guy was. Her mouth curved into a smile.

"I'd love some. Thanks. Let me pay for my books first, and I'll meet you there."

Sweeping an arm out toward the front of the store, he motioned for her to go first.

"I shall wait for you."

Throwing him a quick smile, she got in line, hoping it wouldn't take long to pay for her books. For once, there were enough employees behind the counters. Checkout went quickly and she met up with her good Samaritan.

"What kind of coffee would you like?"

Torie always got flustered trying to make decisions at coffee shops. There were so many to choose from and she never could decide what she wanted, unlike everyone else who rattled off complicated mixtures. The man asking the question now upped the ante. Looking up at the lighted sign on the wall, she noticed the highlighted special.

"The Spiced Gingerbread Cappuccino sounds interesting." She crossed her fingers in hopes that it was a decent choice.

Walking to the counter to place their orders, he turned back to her.

"Would you mind getting a table for us? I will be there shortly with our drinks."

As Torie glanced around the crowded room, her gaze locked on a table that was being vacated. She hurried over, cleaned up after the couple who'd left everything behind, and disposed of the trash. In the few minutes she had to wait for the handsome stranger to join her, she tried to regain her composure and get her act together.

She was acting like a schoolgirl, for crying out loud.

It had been such a long time since she had any social interaction with a man, she was sorely out of practice and nervous. As he neared the table, she once again marveled at him. He was drop-dead gorgeous. This stranger was everything she'd ever fantasized about when it came to the perfect man. Now she would find out if his personality matched the outside. She sighed.

A woman could only hope.

He carefully placed their coffees on the table and sat across from her. The table and chairs weren't small, yet he seemed to dwarf everything around him. Not only was he a big man, but his presence seemed to add *more* to his already dominating size.

"My name is Quinn McGrath, and you are?" He introduced himself with a heart-melting smile.

Flustered by his sensuous smile, Torie bit her lip before returning the introduction.

"I'm Torie Masters. Thank you for the coffee... and again for your help earlier."

"Not a problem, believe me. I am glad I was in the right place at the right time."

To her relief, their conversation went smoothly. She'd never been very good at small talk. He kept the conversational flow going by asking questions and listening intently to her answers. Torie discovered that Quinn, like her, was an avid reader. He preferred mysteries and a little science fiction, having several favorite authors in both genres. From books, they ventured to movies and music. She was continually surprised at how much they had in common. The conversation between them flowed easily and the banter was light and casual, making the time pass quickly.

When Torie heard her phone chime with a text, she checked it hastily. She'd heard the faint chime a couple of times before but had ignored it. She'd been enjoying her conversation too much to want to be interrupted. Figuring her daughter was going to be persistent until she replied, she tapped out a quick answer. Looking at the clock on her phone screen, she was astonished to find that more than two hours had passed. She noticed a slight look of disappointment flitting across Quinn's handsome face as she checked the messages.

"Do you have to go?"

"No, not at all. My daughter is checking on me. I'm not usually out this long," she confessed.

"Excellent. Could I persuade you to have dinner with me? I am enjoying your company and I really am not ready for our time together to end."

Torie's initial reaction was to thank him politely and decline the invitation, but she hesitated. Here was a super attractive man who seemed genuinely interested in her. They had spent the last two hours caught up in captivating conversation.

Why not have dinner with him? What could it possibly hurt?

It had been way too long since she'd enjoyed the company of a man. She was going to do this.

"I realize we do not know each other yet." Quinn must have understood her hesitancy. "There is a steak house right across the parking lot, we can walk over there to have dinner. You will not be far from your vehicle." He placed his hand over hers briefly. "Would that make you feel a little more secure?"

Didn't that just seal the deal?

"I would really like that. Thank you." She accepted his invitation with a gracious smile.

Quinn cleared away their coffee cups. Coming back to the table, he reached for her purchases.

"Would you like to put these in your vehicle before we go to the restaurant?"

"That would be great. My truck is right out front." Feeling like he was reading her mind, she readily agreed.

With a hand on the small of her back, Quinn escorted her out of the bookstore and to her SUV. She stashed her bag in the back with her other purchases before making sure it was locked. They walked through the still-full parking lot to Vincent's Restaurant. It was one of her favorite places to eat. The aroma of grilled steaks and freshly baked bread filled the air, greeting them before they reached the door.

Entering the dimly lit, crowded eatery threw Torie's assaulted senses into overload. The dining area echoed with laughter, music, plates clanging, and murmured conversations. Trying to acclimate to the soft lighting and not get crushed by the crowd was a challenge.

Quinn took charge immediately, using his body to protect her from the hordes of people rushing around them. He put an arm around her shoulders, drawing her close. It was all Torie could do not to melt right into Quinn's side.

He's so very strong... and rock solid... and his scent... what was that? Sandalwood, sage, both? It was glorious, whatever it was.

She wanted to stay right where she was, drinking him in.

Quinn flashed a charming smile at the hostess, and they were quickly led to their seats. Torie wondered how it happened so fast, considering there was a group of people standing around the entrance, obviously on a wait list. She saw the young woman beaming up at Quinn, trying her best to be flirtatious. Torie smiled to herself. She couldn't blame the attendant for trying. If it got them a table, then more power to her and Quinn.

Pulling out a chair for her, Quinn waited until she settled in her seat before taking his own chair.

Brownie points for manners.

He ran his hand lightly over Torie's shoulders as he walked by. She indulged in an inward thrill at his touch, grateful she hadn't been wearing a jacket or coat that would have hampered the feel of his caress. As much as she enjoyed colder weather, the winters in southern Louisiana were usually mild.

"Is this to your liking?" Quinn asked, pulling her from her thoughts.

"Yes, it's fine," she replied, still amazed at how quickly they had been seated.

A server came up immediately to take their drink orders, leaving them for a few minutes to go over their menus, and make their choices. Finding out how akin their preferences were in other areas, it wasn't all that surprising to discover they had similar tastes in food and how it was prepared. The conversation quickly picked up where it had left off at the bookstore. She found out that he was a financial consultant and owned his own business, McGrath Consulting. His brother, who had a corporate law background, was his partner. Quinn was looking for office space in the New Orleans, and surrounding areas, which had led him to Torie's hometown.

Their conversation paused when the server returned with their meals. As the food was placed in front of them, Quinn assured the server that everything was fine, and the young man left them to enjoy their meal. Resuming their talk, Quinn questioned her about her job.

Torie was a little abashed to admit she was just a receptionist. He was quick to quash the *just* part of her job description. When he spoke to her, she felt like she was important, that what she did counted. Torie knew he was right. She did a lot more than simply answer phones and take messages, though seldom did anyone think of it that way, especially her boss.

Over their meal, Quinn regaled her with stories of his childhood in Scotland. Torie was fascinated. She'd always dreamed of visiting Scotland but didn't think she would ever get the chance to travel. He had a way of telling stories that took her there, making her visualize the lovely scenery and the antics of two young brothers growing up in the Highlands.

"I have to say, for growing up in Scotland you don't have much of an accent," she observed between bites.

"It is true. It has faded over time." Quinn nodded. "I have been away from Scotland for many years now. I have traveled the world several times over. When you have had as many business dealings as I have with people of different cultures you tend to lose the accent.

"Dinna fash yirsel lassie. Ah kin pull it oot whin a'm needin' it." Aiming a disarming smile her way, he spoke in a thick Scottish brogue, capping it off by throwing her a roguish wink.

"Yes, indeed, you can. It's still there." Torie laughed in delight.

Lingering over coffee after their meal, Torie glanced around the room. It dawned on her that only a few patrons remained.

"I guess we better call it a night. They'll be closing on us pretty soon."

"Time seems to have gotten away from me today." Quinn reluctantly agreed. "I will walk you back to your vehicle."

They wound their way through the tables, to make their way outside. Taking her hand, Quinn escorted Torie back to her truck.

"Is there a chance I can see you tomorrow? I do not wish to rush you, but there is a reason for my asking."

"What do you mean?" Torie regarded him quizzically.

"I am going to be out of town for the next two weeks on business. I have really enjoyed my time with you today and I want to see you again before I have to leave," Quinn explained. "Please say yes."

"How can I possibly say no to that?" She smiled brightly.

"Excellent!" Quinn replied with a broad grin. "Lunch, then?"

"Lunch, it is." Laughing, Torie nodded.

After exchanging phone numbers, Torie got into her SUV. In her rearview mirror, she could see Quinn stand in place as he watched her drive off, then slowly walk to his own car.

Torie drove home in a daze.

Who knew that today would be the stuff dreams were made of?

Parking her truck under the carport, she heard the chime that let her know she had a text message. Glancing down at her cell phone, she saw it was from Quinn.

Thank you for today. I look forward to seeing you tomorrow. ~Q.

Hugging herself, she knew she was going to have the most pleasant of dreams that night.

CLAIMING MAGICK

Madison Granger

Chapter 1

Havenport, 1935

"You promised! You pledged yourself to me, and now you think to break your vow?"

Sarah Murphy's blood ran cold. How could he do this to her after all this time? She hid her hands in the folds of her skirt to conceal the tremors. The room was suddenly hot, and she couldn't breathe.

"Sarah, be reasonable," Jeremy pleaded. He never moved from the center of the room, only stood there, watching her from a distance.

"Reasonable, is it?" Sarah screeched. "For five years, I have waited for you, listened to your promises and sweet words. Now, you want to call it off like I was never anything to you?" She wanted to throw herself at him, and rake out his eyes, but she faced him as his words cut her heart to shreds.

"She's my Fated Mate. I can't turn my back on her. She's the one I'm meant to be with."

"What about me? Am I nothing to you? What am I supposed to do now? I'll be the laughingstock of Havenport. I'll never be able to show my face again." She wouldn't be able to walk along the town's streets. They would stare and point, and she wouldn't be able to bear the shame.

"I care for you, but she's my mate," Jeremy pressed. Trying another tactic, he hurried on. "People forget quickly, Sarah. You're overreacting, surely."

Sarah slapped Jeremy. The sting burned her fingers, leaving a glaring red handprint on his freshly shaven face.

"Overreacting, indeed! You'll live to regret this decision, Jeremy Reed." How dare he choose a mangy dog over her, a young, beautiful, and powerful witch? He would live to rue this day!

"Please, Sarah! How was I to know Jenny would come into my life? I didn't plan any of it to work out this way." Jeremy covered his cheek with a shaky hand. "Don't do anything foolish or something you'll regret. I know how you are when you feel you've been slighted."

Sarah stared at him in shock. He had the nerve...

"Slighted? I may have been slighted?" Her laugh was bordering on hysterical, breaking off on a sob. "I can promise, anything I do to you I won't regret for a minute."

"You have to understand. I did it for the good of the pack." He held out a hand to her.

Sarah slapped his hand away. "The pack... always the pack." She spat the words back at him. "That's what this is truly about. You were never planning on making me your wife. The pack wouldn't accept a witch. Oh, no. Now that you are Alpha, you had to find a suitable wife, another wolf like you."

Jeremy tugged on his sleeves and adjusted his collar. Pulling his timepiece from his pocket, he glanced at his watch.

"I have to go; I have other business to attend. Once again, I'm sorry to have distressed you, but my mind is made up. I'm going to take Jenny as my mate. I wish you only the best."

Sarah watched him leave without another word. Her hopes and dreams were shattered, crumbling into dust to be blown away by the four winds. How would she hold her head up after word got out she'd been jilted? She'd be laughed at behind her back—and knowing most of the town's women, they wouldn't be that discreet, they would laugh in front of her. She wouldn't be able to endure it. She had to do something!

Wrapping a shawl around her shoulders, she ventured into the cool night. Looking up, she was reminded it was a full moon. The Lady's silver glow seemed unusually bright. Her magick would be strong. Sarah sniffed. She would use it to her advantage. Hurrying back inside, she gathered what she would need.

Sarah carefully crushed the herbs she'd gathered, mixing them in a small bowl. Lighting her candles, she dipped the flame into the herbs, watching them hiss and crackle. Raising her hands and her voice, she called upon the goddesses of wrath and vengeance.

For the cruelty and the pain,
you have brought to me,
I turn the tables three times three.
When dusk comes through,
bringing light to your deed,
my curse upon you and all your seed.
I say this spell tonight,
I am witch. I stand and fight.

It was done. Jeremy Reed and his line would diminish... slowly but surely.

Chapter 2

Havenport, Present Day

Rowan Murphy heard the bell tinkle over the door, then her cat, Jinx, hissed, and a familiar voice called out.

"Buster, come here! You bad boy, come to Mama right this instant!"

What a wonderful start to a morning, Mrs. Rogers and her designer dog, Buster. Rowan rolled her eyes. *How many times had she asked that woman to leave the dog at home?* Preparing for the inevitable, she hastily redid her messy bun, silver tendrils framing her face. Anxious amethyst eyes stared back at her in the oval office mirror.

The crash was expected. So were the flurry of fur and the hissing, spitting fury of her cat. What Rowan didn't expect was the amount of damage done in the short time it took to get to the chaos, grab Jinx, and fend off the pint-sized demon dog. Baskets of crystals lay scattered along the long counter and floor, a small display case holding small jars of ointments had been knocked over, glass containers rolling away or broken, and small bags of incense were everywhere. She barely caught the statue of the Morrigan before it crashed to the floor.

"Mrs. Rogers, what did I tell you about bringing Buster into the store?" Rowan desperately tried to keep her voice calm, with an arm around a hissing Jinx and the Morrigan in her other hand. She tried to keep a pleasant smile on her face, but this one particular patron was a true test of her patience, to say the least.

"Oh, Rowan, you know I can't leave Buster at home. He would be so lonely. Wouldn't you be lonely, Mama's little baby boy?" She rained kisses on the little dog, who stared defiantly at Rowan.

Rowan was mentally going through her spellbooks for something that would work on small, spoiled, ankle-biters when the owner caught her attention.

"Did the amulet come in yet, dear?"

"The amulet? Oh, yes, I have it locked away in my office. Give me a minute and I'll get it for you." Rowan hurried to her office, once again reminding herself this was the very reason she put up with Mrs. Rogers and her irritating dog. By herself, the woman spent enough money in her shop to keep it running. Rowan couldn't afford to offend, much less alienate, the older woman.

"You need to stop antagonizing that demon dog. Stay in here for a while," she fussed at Jinx as she set him free on the small loveseat. She went behind her desk to a framed picture on the wall, and with a practiced spin, Rowan opened the safe. Carefully removing the slender box, she removed the lid, making sure nothing had happened to the necklace. It had been locked in the safe, away from harm, but stranger things had happened before.

Bringing the antique amulet to the counter, she showed it to Mrs. Rogers for her approval.

"At last! I've wanted this for so long," she stage-whispered to Rowan as if it was a huge secret. "I never thought Mr. Rourke would ever give it up, and at such a bargain, too!"

A bargain, indeed! Rourke had doubled the price of the amulet before he parted with it. The man held no sentimental value to his pieces. *He's in it for the profit.* Placing the lid back on the box, Rowan slid it into a bag and wrote out the receipt, making sure she added in the damage to her supplies and shop.

Mrs. Rogers reached into her purse, a wallet stuffed with receipts and cards, pulled one out without even looking at it, and handed it to Rowan.

"I'll pay for the damage to your shop, of course."

She never met Rowan's stare, still busy cuddling her traumatized baby. The sale was approved, and Rowan did a mental fist pump. Rent was covered for this month and next. Of course, she would have to make more ointment to replace the ones destroyed, but this way, she'd been paid for them. Once the older woman, with Buster in tow, left the shop, Rowan looked upward, a smirk on her face, as she called out.

"You can come out now. The coast is clear, and you both have cleanup duty."

A young woman with flaming-red, spiral curls and green eyes slipped into the room, quietly joined by a young man with a mop of unruly black hair and crystal blue eyes. Amy and Jason, Rowan's shop assistants, showed a lot of potential except when it came to dealing with the more difficult customers, like Mrs. Rogers. Then they whipped out their invisible capes, and she was on her own.

"Sorry, Ro, but I was in the bathroom," Amy apologized with a giggle. "Some things can't be rushed."

Rowan arched a brow in Jason's direction.

"In my defense, I was in the back, unpacking boxes," Jason declared. "You were already dealing with her before I even knew she was here."

"You are both in the clear… this time." Rowan sighed. "But you need to learn how to deal with these women. As unpleasant as they and their animals are, they keep us afloat, and thanks to today's sale, we're floating quite nicely," she said with a smile, her irritation with the situation lifting instantly.

"Did someone say pizza?" Jason favored her with his best lopsided grin.

"I don't recall saying anything at all about food." Rowan laughed in spite of herself. "But I think we can manage a pizza for lunch."

"I want pineapple!" Amy called dibs.

"You had it last time," Jason complained.

"You two work it out. One pizza only," she warned. "I have work to do in my office. Clean up that disaster and try to keep the place intact and running."

"Yes, ma'am," Amy and Jason chorused.

Rowan sat at her desk, staring at the desktop screen for a moment. Her wallpaper was a photo taken when she was a child. It was a shot of her grandparent's house on a hazy summer day, with a rope swing hung from an old oak in the front yard. If you looked past the house, you could make out the barn in the back. She missed it all—her grandparents, the house, the horses.

She'd had a memorable childhood, and it stemmed from that one place. She blew her bangs up in a huff. It was all gone now. The only thing keeping her going was her dream that one day she would buy back the piece of property her grandfather had sold. It wouldn't bring her childhood, or her grandparents back, but she wanted the house and the land. It had sentimental value. A piece of her heart was there, and it was all she wanted.

Rowan sat back, looking out the window at nothing. She needed to take the picture down and bury those memories. Every day, she saw the picture, and it was the same thing—pleasant memories, a yearning wish for what once was, and more fuel to the hatred burning in her heart. It was eating her alive, and the worst part was she knew it, and it truly wasn't justified.

It wasn't their fault, not really. They bought the land. She shouldn't hate them, but she did. She hated the shifters for taking what should have been hers.

ZANE

Book One of The Bayou Crescent Wolves

Madison Granger

Chapter 1

"You're actually going to do this?" Amber stopped midstride, a hand on her hip, as she shot Zane an incredulous look.

"What? Are you kidding me?" Zane ran a hand through his short black hair, tugging at the ends in frustration. "We've been through this. You didn't want to stay with the Crossroads pack, and you've done nothing but cause trouble in Bayou Crescent. This is your only option, Amber." He glared at her until she dropped her gaze. "You agreed to the transfer. It's too late to turn back now."

Amber eased up to him, her hand trailing up his arm. She bit her bottom lip, giving him a pleading look with large, dark brown eyes.

"I always thought you and I would hook up."

"You knew better than that from the start." Zane closed his eyes, praying for patience. "You're not my Fated Mate, and I don't play those games." He moved away from her touch and gestured toward the two-story, rustic office. "Come on, the Alpha is waiting for us, and I, for one, don't plan on making him angry."

With a long-suffering sigh, Amber walked alongside him. Zane opened the door, and she strode past him, throwing herself onto a chair. Rolling his eyes, Zane ignored her and made his way to the receptionist, introducing himself and stating their business. Within minutes, they were shown to a large, masculine office.

Steven Woodward sat behind a polished antique walnut desk. Opened books stacked atop one another took up more than half of the available space, leaving barely enough room for the computer and phone. As they entered, the Alpha rose, skirting the desk to warmly shake Zane's hand.

"My apologies for not being here yesterday to greet you. Pack business had me out of town longer than I anticipated. I hope your accommodations were to your satisfaction?"

"No apology is necessary. Pack business is priority." A look of understanding passed between them. "Your staff saw to our every need and comfort. I wish I had more time to visit. I'd like to discuss your secret of keeping everything so organized, especially in your absence."

"Careful selection and loyalty." Steven chuckled under his breath. "It wasn't always this way. It's taken me years to reach this level of trust and management." He glanced at Amber, who was fixedly staring out the window. "I assume this is our new member?"

"Amber." Zane's jaw clenched when the female refused to acknowledge him.

A wave of power charged the air, and Amber whined, baring her neck in submission. Zane felt the power, but being an alpha himself, didn't feel the impulse to submit.

"Amber Gardner, your acceptance into this pack hinges on your respect, adherence to the laws I lay down, and your submission. Do you understand?" The pack leader's eyes glowed a brilliant gold, his voice a low growl filling the room with authority.

"Yes, Alpha, I understand." A sheen of perspiration covered the omega's face, her hands clenching the arms of the chair. She gasped, slumping back in the chair when Steven pulled in his power, releasing her from its hold.

Woodward nodded in satisfaction, turning his attention back to Zane.

"She'll be fine. Once she's settled and acquainted with our ways, we'll find her a suitable job, and she'll become a contributing pack member."

Zane didn't miss the shocked look in Amber's eyes and bit back harsh laughter. The omega was in for a rude awakening, and he was sorry he wouldn't be there to see it.

"Thank you for helping us out." Zane shook Steven's hand firmly. "If it wouldn't have been for Maddox steering us in your direction..."

"Don't worry about it." The Denver Alpha leaned in closer and whispered in Zane's ear. "I've had a fair amount of experience with this kind of problem. She's better off here."

The knowing look in Woodward's eyes settled any misgivings Zane had about dumping the omega onto another pack.

Turning, Zane caught Amber's gaze, raking him up and down, her dark eyes smoldering and a wicked tongue licking her full, ripe lips. He frowned as he walked out of the Denver pack leader's office. The she-wolf didn't get it... she would, though, soon enough.

Amber had been one of a dozen or more omegas who had been abused by their pack alpha. Rescued by Rafe Martin, leader of the Crossroads pack, Amber had swiftly realized the fit wasn't a good one in the family-oriented clan and had asked to be allowed to join the Bayou Crescent wolves. It hadn't taken Zane or his brothers long to figure out there was no pack in Louisiana who would ever satisfy Amber. Even though she was an omega, she was restless and prone to drama, stirring up trouble on a daily basis.

Thanks to Maddox Ward, Alpha of the NOLA Shifters and his network of packs in the U.S., he'd been able to set up the transfer for Amber to move to

Denver. Their pack was larger than all the packs in Louisiana put together, and Amber would have her choice of unmated males to play with. As long as she didn't play her games with the mated ones, she'd be fine.

If she kept up her little tricks, however, she'd find herself up against an alpha who brooked no tolerance with troublesome omegas. If Amber didn't toe the line here, she'd find herself packless… and even she knew the consequences of such a fate.

Striding across the parking area to his rental, Zane felt a sense of relief this was finally behind him. His timing couldn't have been more perfect. By the time he got to the airport, he wouldn't have long to wait for his flight. He wasn't crazy about flying, not many shifters were. He would have preferred to make the trip to Denver on his bike, regardless of the distance, but there was no way he would go anywhere with Amber clutched to his backside. She would have taken full advantage of the situation and no doubt, they would have ended up wrecked somewhere between Louisiana and Colorado. The flight was a no-brainer.

Once on the plane, Zane pulled out a paperback he'd bought at the airport on the trip in. Figuring if his nose was buried in a book, Amber would leave him alone. The ruse had worked, for the most part. When she realized he wasn't going to talk to her more than what was necessary, she'd resorted to watching a movie on her tablet.

His choice of book was regrettable, but he was committed to it, and had started reading. The picture of a wolf on the cover had caught his eye. He'd picked it up without skimming the synopsis on the back cover, much less paying attention to the title. Turned out, it was one of the paranormal romances that seemed to be all the rage these days.

Since he was already more than halfway through the story, he figured he might as well finish it. It wasn't a horrible book, just not accurate. What shifter story would be? Their secret was top priority and would remain that way for the unforeseeable future.

"Are you enjoying the book?" The low-pitched, provocative voice held more than a hint of humor.

Zane looked up to find the flight attendant smiling at him, her eyes dancing with mirth. Heat coursed up his neck, and he fingered the collar of his shirt.

"Not my usual read. I picked it up by accident." He shrugged, a corner of his mouth tugging into a smile. "I was bored, figured I'd give it a shot."

"It's actually a rather good story." She winked at him, openly flirting. "The author is one of my favorites. You should read some of her other works."

"Um, yeah, I'll look into it." *That would be a definite no.*

"Is there anything I can get for you?" The attendant leaned over him, giving him a view of generous breasts straining against the fabric of her uniform.

"No, I'm fine. Thanks." Zane had nowhere to go. She was practically on top of him, and her perfume was speedily giving him a headache. "It's a short flight. I'm good."

She unhurriedly straightened as she made one last attempt.

"If you change your mind, my name is Carol."

"Appreciate it." Zane waved the book and winked at her. "Need to finish this before we land."

With a smile, she moved on to check on the other passengers.

Zane leaned against the seat, breathing easier now she was gone. The flight attendant was an attractive woman, and no doubt, he could have spent a few hours of pleasure with her, but she wasn't his type, and he had other things on his mind than a quick dalliance with a human.

Opening the paperback, he made himself focus on the pages, blocking out the passengers around him and the fact he was in a metal can flying way too high above the ground.

When the landing announcement came, Zane closed the book with a snap, tossing it on the empty seat beside him. He'd finished it but would leave it for someone else to pass the time.

Zane wasted no time, grabbing his carry-on and heading for the garage parking lot. Not having luggage to claim saved him aggravation, and he started up the black Ford Raptor with a grunt of satisfaction. The roar of the engine echoing in the enclosed area, he eased out of the parking bay, making his way to the highway and home.

Squinting against the harsh sunlight, Zane slipped on his aviator sunglasses and kicked on the air conditioning. It would take a few minutes before the air cooled, but it would be worth the wait. Summer in south Louisiana was always a scorcher, and while he was used to the heat and humidity, he'd be lying if he said he didn't appreciate air conditioning.

Zane tapped a button on the steering wheel. "Call Ridge," he growled at the voice-activated multimedia system. He may have been raised down in the bayou, living a simple life, but he did love technology and all the gadgets that came with it.

"Made it back in one piece, brother?" Ridge's soft Cajun cadence was a balm to Zane's ears. His ties to Bayou Crescent and his brothers were strong, and Zane was more at peace when he was home.

"Yeah, I'm on Highway 90. Should be there in an hour or so."

"Good deal. Try to avoid any more speeding tickets." Ridge sniggered, knowing darn well Zane had a heavy foot, especially since he'd bought the new truck. "Everything go okay in Denver?"

"As well as could be expected. We owe Maddox a big favor, though. You know that, right?"

Zane waited patiently for his brother's response. Ridge weighed each word before he spoke. Some saw it as a flaw or defect until he said his piece. Ridge wasn't slow—he was careful.

"I know, and it's been discussed. I'll take care of it when it's time."

Zane knew better than to press him. Ridge would talk when he was good and ready, and only if he thought Zane needed to know.

"You always do, bro. I'm going to duck off and grab some lunch at Sparh's before I head home. I missed breakfast and my stomach is rumbling." The popular seafood restaurant was in a prime location between Bayou Crescent and New Orleans, on a stretch of highway with no competitors nearby.

"Order a takeout for me and Cole," Ridge requested, a hint of laughter in the deep rumble. "I could go for a seafood platter."

"If you'd get out of the bayou once in a while, you could try some of these restaurants."

"Why? You're there already. Bring some home. Drive carefully, Zane."

The line went dead, and Zane snorted. Typical Ridge.

An hour later, his belly full, and the truck smelling like all kinds of seafood heaven, thanks to the two large to-go bags on the floorboard, Zane eased back onto the highway. A nap sounded better than the drive home, but he'd wasted enough time and was eager to get back to Bayou Crescent.

About the Author

Madison Granger is a free-spirited late bloomer. She stubbornly lives by three beliefs: dreams can come true, never give up, and you're never too old to try new things. She is living proof of all three adages, vowing she isn't done by a long shot.

Born and raised near New Orleans and even closer to the swamps of south Louisiana, Madison is no stranger to tales of the magical and different.

Madison loves to read, listen to music (mostly country, with a little alternative thrown in), thrives on coffee, and has had a life-long love of horses. She collects dragons, gargoyles, and angels... and anything else that catches her fancy.

Madison's stories are touched by magic and revolve around sexy Alphas, curvy, strong-willed heroines, and always have a Happy Ever After.

Madison welcomes stalkers… well, the book kind anyway, and would love for you to join her journey.

Website

https://www.MadisonGranger.com/

Facebook

https://www.facebook.com/MadisonGrangerAuthor/

Amazon

https://www.amazon.com/author/madisongranger

Goodreads

https://www.goodreads.com/author/show/15139766.Madison_Granger

Bookbub

https://www.bookbub.com/authors/madison-granger

Made in the USA
Columbia, SC
16 August 2024

40076252R10134